RISSA BARTHOLOMEW'S

DECLARATION of INDEPENDENCE

by Lynda B. Comerford

SCHOLASTIC PRESS • New York

This book could never have been written without the support
of the following people:
Rosie Brill, Carol Parish, Diane Roback, and all the
Comerfords. With deep appreciation to Nancy Gallt and
Kara LaReau for their patience, encouragement, and
tremendous insight.

Text copyright © 2009 by Lynda B. Comerford
All rights reserved. Published by Scholastic Press, an imprint of Scholastic Inc., *Publishers since 1920.* SCHOLASTIC, SCHOLASTIC PRESS, and associated logos are trademarks and/or registered trademarks of Scholastic Inc.
No part of this publication may be reproduced, stored in a retrieval system, or transmitted in any form or by any means, electronic, mechanical, photocopying, recording, or otherwise, without written permission of the publisher. For information regarding permission, write to Scholastic Inc., Attention: Permissions Department, 557 Broadway, New York, NY 10012.
Library of Congress Cataloging-in-Publication Data
Comerford, Lynda B.
Rissa Bartholomew's declaration of independence / Lynda B. Comerford. -- 1st ed.
p. cm.
Summary: Having told off all of her old friends at her eleventh birthday party, Rissa starts middle school determined to make new friends while being herself, not simply being part of a "herd."
ISBN-13: 978-0-545-05058-6
ISBN-10: 0-545-05058-8
[1. Identity–Fiction. 2. Self-actualization (Psychology)–Fiction. 3. Friendship–Fiction. 4. Middle schools–Fiction. 5. Schools–Fiction. 6. Family life–Illinois–Fiction. 7. Illinois–Fiction.] I. Title.
PZ7.C73194Ris 2009   [Fic]–dc22   2008026618
10 9 8 7 6 5 4 3 2 1   09 10 11 12 13
Printed in the U.S.A.   23
First edition, May 2009
Book design by Elizabeth B. Parisi

TO BONNIE BRILL

CHAPTER 1

THE STORY OF FERDINAND

Five years ago, when I was in first grade, our teacher read us this book about a bull named Ferdinand. He was different from all the other bulls because he liked to hang out by himself instead of running around with his herd, doing bull stuff, like butting heads and snorting a lot. Even when old Ferdinand had his chance to be a superstar by winning a bullfight, he *refused* to do what any bull in his right mind would do. He wouldn't paw the dirt or act tough. He just stood in the ring sniffing flowers, doing what he wanted to do instead of doing what the other bulls thought he *ought* to do. Of course this story had a lesson. Books read aloud by teachers always do. What we were supposed to learn was that it's okay to do your own thing and not follow the herd.

It seems like every chance they get, grown-ups are pounding you with that message. "Be true to yourself," they say.

"Dare to be different!" They make it sound so easy, like it's something just about everyone would want to do so they can turn out to be like Ferdinand, who went on to be loved and admired by all. But here is something that grown-ups will never tell you. Being your own person doesn't always make you a hero. I know on account of what happened to me this year when I started middle school.

CHAPTER 2

NOT TWO PEAS IN A POD

Deciding to be independent wasn't something that just happened out of the blue. Looking back, I realize that it was something that had been in the back of my mind for a while, especially in the summer after fifth grade. Then, like almost every kid I knew, I was part of a "herd," unlike old Ferdinand the bull. Mine was made up of me and four girls who went to my school: Beth White, Jayne Littleton, Kerry McGrew, and Angel Franzetti. The reason we ended up together didn't have much to do with the fact we had a bunch of stuff in common. It had more to do with the fact we all lived in the same part of town and our mothers got together and arranged a car pool. If riding squished together in the back of a minivan doesn't make you part of a herd, I don't know what does.

In the herd, I was most connected to Beth White, probably because I'd known her the longest. Actually, I'd known her forever. By some stroke of really weird luck, we were born on the same day in the same hospital to mothers who knew each other from high school. Mom and Mrs. White hadn't stayed in touch over the years, so it was like this big reunion for them when they bumped into each other in the maternity ward. Then Mom and Mrs. White became friends again, the Whites moved into a house a few blocks away from us, and everyone expected Beth and me to be best friends like them. Nobody ever asked our permission.

Sometimes I used to imagine our moms planning it all out on the day they met in the hospital. The conversation probably would have gone something like this:

MOM: Catherine! What have you been doing all of these years since high school?

MRS. WHITE: I've married a rich husband, what about you?

MOM: Nothing much.

MRS. WHITE: Aren't our daughters beautiful?

MOM: Yes. (She's looking at me, the bald, scrawny baby.)

MRS. WHITE: Don't you just know these girls are going to be best friends?

MOM: (No comment. She is too busy thinking about the advantages of Beth's and my future friendship. We could share toys. No use having two swing sets or two sandboxes or two playhouses, and maybe the Whites could buy some of the bigger, more expensive stuff.)

MRS. WHITE: Let's start setting up playdates right away!

MOM: (enthusiastically) Great idea!

To be fair, Beth did turn out to be a pretty cool friend for most of her life. Here are some reasons why:

★ 1. She was generally a very honest person and never cheated at Monopoly (unlike my sister, Mary Ann, who used to hide $500 bills in the bathroom).

★ 2. She loved animals as much as I did and always used to let me play with her cat, Motormouth, since my mom wouldn't let me have a pet of my own.

★ 3. When she was really excited, Beth's eyes lit up and her smile got really big and sometimes she actually started trembling so that you couldn't help but be excited, too.

When we were little, Beth and I spent a ton of time together. In winter, we built forts and played "Eskimos caught in a blizzard." In summer, we rode bikes down the Constitution Trail and looked for diamonds and rubies that might have gotten mixed in with the gravel along the side of the path. Most weekends, we watched Saturday morning cartoons together, and when we outgrew cartoons, we started watching the Saturday Night Creature Feature on channel 10. Sometimes we got into fights, but most of the time we got along pretty well.

But things started to be different at the end of fifth grade, and I got the feeling that sometimes Beth's mind was on other things besides what we were doing when we were together. For example, during a really exciting part of a Creature Feature, Beth might say something like, "Do you think I should get my hair highlighted?" and I'd miss an important scene. Or during a game of Monopoly, she'd want to discuss which boy on the school soccer team was cutest, instead of making up her mind about whether she wanted to trade Park Place for all my railroads.

And once, when we were over at my house making ice-cream sundaes, Beth suddenly announced, "I want everyone to call me Bethany instead of Beth from now on."

I stopped licking sauce off my spoon and stared at her, trying to imagine her as a Bethany. I couldn't. Beth was no more a Bethany than I was a Clarissa, which is the name my mother (who must have gone temporarily insane) wrote down on my birth certificate.

"What's the matter with the name Beth?" I asked.

"It's too ordinary and babyish."

Babyish? That didn't make sense. Beth was named after her grandmother, who was over sixty years old. Nobody called *her* Bethany. She was Grandma Beth.

"I don't know," I said. "Bethany doesn't sound right. The only person who calls you that is your mom when she's really mad at you."

"Jayne, Kerry, and Angel call me Bethany," she informed me.

I shrugged my shoulders and mumbled something about trying to remember to call her Bethany, but I knew I'd have a hard time doing it.

I don't know why Beth wanting to change her name bothered me so much, but it did, and there were other things that bothered me, too. I started to be annoyed by some of Beth's little habits, like the way she pouted when she didn't get her way and the way she walked around like a ballerina with her back stiff and her feet turned out so everyone would know she took dance lessons. Then I'd be reminded of some other irritating things about her — things that weren't even her fault — like how she was an only child, and was and probably always will be taller than me. Then there was the thing about the clothes.

When I was really little, Mom used to make my clothes while Beth wore designer-brand dungarees and little

T-shirts with alligators on the front. Then in about the second grade, I figured out that labels saying "Lovingly made by Annie Bartholomew" just didn't cut it. So I complained that I wanted clothes like Beth's. And that's just what I got. Not *new* shirts and jeans, like I was hoping, but boxes of Beth's old hand-me-downs, which Mrs. White personally delivered. Most of the clothes were limp with wear and didn't fit quite right. But Mom, who believed "high-quality clothing should not go to waste," starched them up, took in seams, and made me wear them.

Okay, okay. I know I'm getting off the subject and that hand-me-down thing is really more about our mothers, but you get the picture of how Beth was making me miserable. It was like all the good things about her had started to shrink down in size and all of the bad things about her were growing bigger and bigger. I don't know whose fault it was that it was happening. It just was, and it suddenly dawned on me that Beth and I weren't the "two peas in a pod" that our mothers and everyone else thought we were. In fact, I had trouble thinking of any ways we were the same.

CHAPTER 3

TAGGING ALONG

All that summer, I went back and forth between being mad at Beth and feeling guilty because I was mad at her, but I never said a word about how I felt. I kept hoping that I'd wake up one morning and things would go back to normal, and Beth would be the friend I liked instead of this irritating person who kept asking to be called Bethany.

Things didn't get better, though. Beth continued to get on my nerves, especially when she decided she was "too old" for board games and kept pushing me to go to the mall with her and the rest of our friends. Her sudden interest in shopping may have been due to the fact her parents started giving her a clothing allowance (which, according to Mom, wasn't going to happen in *our* house until I was in high school).

Trying to be a good sport, I usually followed Beth to the mall to meet up with the rest of our group. I felt pretty stupid, though, like a tagalong, and straggled behind the rest of the group as they went from store to store to flip through racks of jeans and spin carousels of earrings. The other girls in our group kept themselves entertained, but I got restless pretty quickly. If you ask me, there is nothing more boring in the world than wandering aimlessly around a shopping center when there's no possibility of you actually *buying* anything because you have a closet full of "high-quality" hand-me-downs and just enough money for a hot pretzel.

On days when the other girls couldn't hang out at the mall because they were busy or broke or both, Beth *still* dragged me there to do what she called "research." This meant spending a good amount of time near the entrance of Studio 99, a store where high school and college kids with a lot of money shop. Beth would sit on the mall bench and watch the older girls going in and coming out of the store. It was like she was playing detective or something, trying to figure out how to look and act like a teenager. You could tell she was just dying to be one and in fact kept a little spiral notebook to jot down beauty tips and fashion ideas and to count down the days until she turned thirteen. Every once in a while, just to test her, I'd say, "How many more days?" and she'd know the answer right off the bat. It used to be a joke between us, but by the end of July, it wasn't so funny anymore.

In the same way I didn't get Beth's new interest in the mall, and her determination to change her name, I didn't get why she was in such a hurry to be a teenager. Personally, I'd *lived* with one — my older sister, Mary Ann — for many years, and I knew for a fact that being one was overrated. Before she went off to college to become an adult, Mary Ann was a very weepy individual, and it made me think that teen life must be pretty hard. I'd seen Mary Ann cry over boys, cry over her grades, cry over pimples, and cry when she hit a parked car the very first day she got her driver's license. I was not looking forward to following in her footsteps.

I tried to explain how nervous I was about becoming a teenager and how I didn't like spending so much time in front of Studio 99, but Beth just didn't get it. There were a lot of things she didn't get about me, I was starting to realize. In fact, there were a few times that summer when she called me a "party pooper," which I assure you could not be further from the truth. I was (and still am) a very fun-loving person, but the problem was that my idea of fun and Beth's idea of fun were becoming way, WAY different. The worst part of it was that the other girls in our group were thinking Beth's way of fun was better than mine.

To be honest, by the end of the summer, it wasn't just Beth who was bugging me. My other friends were, too. I'd started to notice how every conversation I had with Kerry ended up with her telling some story about a gymnastic meet she'd won. When Angel was around, I could hardly get in a word at all because she was becoming the boss of everyone, and since Jayne had gotten braces on her teeth, she'd turned sort of quiet and gloomy, thinking that no boy would ever give her a second look.

And it was like none of the girls (except maybe bossy Angel) could think for themselves anymore. When one of the girls found something she liked at the mall, she had to make sure everyone else liked it, too. Then it usually turned out that everyone (with enough money) ended up buying the same things. Beth, Jayne, Kerry, and Angel had matching daisy earrings, the same kind of sunglasses, and the same brand of capri pants that could be rolled up into shorts. Even if I'd had the money, I wouldn't have bought any of those things. I mean, who wants to look just like everyone else?

Now that I think about it, I guess leaving Beth and the rest of the group was something that was just bound to happen, and I probably *should* have done it the time I got ditched at the Step Ahead shoe store right before I turned eleven.

It was about a week before our double birthday celebration (which happened every year on August 20), and Beth wanted me to go to the mall to help her pick out some new sandals to wear to our party. But of course she needed more than just my opinion. So there we were, Beth, Kerry, Jayne, Angel, and me, sitting inside the Step Ahead shoe store, discussing whether leather or patent leather straps looked better. There were about a million pairs of rejected sandals strewn around us on the floor.

"I like the pink ones." Angel picked up a pair of sandals from off the floor. "Try these on again. They're *so* you, Bethany."

Beth took the sandals, daintily put them on her feet, and started walking around the store, careful to keep her toes turned out. "Do you think they make my toes look fat?" she asked.

Everyone assured her they didn't.

Then, instead of sitting back down, Beth went over to a sale table filled with shoes.

"Hey, you guys, check this out!" She held up a metallic gold shoe with a spiky heel.

"Oh, my God! That's the ugliest thing I've ever seen!" Kerry shrieked.

Then everyone except me went over to the table to investigate, and it became a contest to see who could find the most outrageous pair of all. Shoe boxes fell to the floor. A bow fell off a slipper. Laughter got shriller. Angel tossed a purple sneaker at Beth, narrowly missing her arm. In retaliation, Beth threw a pair of flip-flops at Angel.

"You'd better quit it before we get into trouble," I told the girls.

"We're just messing around. Stop being such a baby," Beth laughed.

Me, a baby? I wasn't the one throwing shoes. I was the one maturely trying to warn everyone to behave themselves before it was too late.

"Hey! You kids!" It was the salesclerk, who had been in the back room trying to find Beth a pair of Birkenstocks in size seven narrow. He trotted toward us with a shoe box under his arm.

"Let's get out of here!" Kerry squealed, and everyone took off running.

Except me. I stood there frozen as the salesman approached, and I was the one who had to take the blame for making a mess of his display. Then I had to listen to his grumblings about "irresponsible behavior" and how "kids shouldn't go anywhere without their parents" as I dutifully picked up shoes off the floor and matched them with their mates.

I was fuming by the time I caught up with Beth and the others, but everyone else thought the whole thing was a big joke, so I swallowed my anger and pretended I thought it was funny, too.

CHAPTER 4

MY NOT-SO-GRACEFUL EXIT

On the day of Beth's and my birthday party, I was still pretty upset about the Step Ahead shoe store incident. But that wasn't the only reason I was in a grumpy mood. Another reason was that Beth called me that morning, a couple of hours before the party, to tell me that she'd gotten her hair highlighted and to describe her new birthday outfit, which included pink sandals (which she'd bought downtown with her mother). As she went on to tell me every detail of what she planned to wear to the party, I was thinking about my favorite shorts, spotted with ink where a pen had exploded in the pocket. Did my mother have time to run them through the washer and dryer before the party? Unlikely.

"So, what are you going to wear?" Beth wanted to know.

"I haven't decided yet. I'm still in my pajamas," I said. And it was the truth.

As soon as I got off the phone, I went upstairs, pulled out every piece of clothing I owned, and piled everything on my bed. Some of my T-shirts were passable, but most of my shorts used to be Beth's, and there was no way I was going to wear any of her stuff to the party and have someone say, "Hey, Rissa, those shorts look familiar. . . . Oh, yeah, Beth used to wear them back in the third grade."

Just as I was about to start digging through my laundry hamper to see if I could find something unstained and not too smelly, Mom yelled up the stairs to tell me to hurry up and finish getting ready for the party because she was ready to leave. She absolutely HATES being late to anything, even a kids' party at Dino's Pizzeria, which was not my choice of location, by the way.

I pulled out the biggest T-shirt I could find and just hoped it was long enough to cover the ink stain on my shorts. When I was finished getting dressed, I ran a comb through my hair and figured I was about as ready as I'd ever be to celebrate turning eleven.

"Why are you in such a bad mood?" Mom asked on our way to the car.

"I'm not in a bad mood," I lied.

"Well, I hope you're not still pouting about having your party at Dino's. They have fried chicken there. I checked. Or you could order pizza without sauce."

You might find it strange that a person like me, who is

allergic to tomatoes and therefore pizza sauce, would be celebrating her birthday at a pizza parlor. Needless to say, it was Beth who came up with the idea because she'd heard from Kerry's older brother, Matt, that Dino's was this "really cool teen hangout." My mom agreed with the plan because Mrs. White agreed, and whatever Mrs. White decided usually ended up happening.

When we arrived at Dino's, it was too hot inside the dining room. It felt like we were inside the pizza oven instead of standing near the front entrance. It was also kind of dark, which made me a little nervous. I've never liked restaurants that are dimly lit. They make me wonder what the manager might be trying to hide, like maybe crumbs left over by a previous customer, or dirty smudges on the silverware, or (and this is what worries me the most) little bugs nesting in a corner, which might, at times, travel to the kitchen to sample the food or crawl into your shoe while you're enjoying your tomatoless meal.

I glanced suspiciously around the restaurant. And I noticed something. There was not one teenager to be seen. In fact, most of the customers were really old.

Beth (with newly highlighted hair) and Mrs. White were already sitting at a long table, which was actually four small tables pushed together. Beth had on her new birthday clothes. Mrs. White looked like she was wearing new clothes, too, and seemed out of place in her expensive-looking polo shirt with matching pearl earrings. She gave me a little wave, said, "Hello, birthday girl!" and started talking to my mother about how this was the first time she'd been to Dino's and it wasn't at all what she expected.

"I like your hair and your new outfit," I told Beth, trying to sneak a peek behind the table to make sure no bugs were hiding.

"Thanks." She glanced down at my shorts. "You have a stain on your pocket," she whispered.

"I do?" I pretended to be surprised.

"Just keep your hands in your lap and nobody will notice."

I sat down and put my hand over the stain to make Beth happy, but I wondered what the big deal was when there was a stain on the carpet underneath the table that was a lot bigger and more noticeable than the one on my shorts.

"Are you sure this place is supposed to be popular? There aren't any teenagers here," I pointed out to Beth. "Maybe Kerry's brother was teasing when he said this was a 'cool hangout.'"

"I don't think so," Beth said firmly, but I disagreed. Matt was always playing tricks to make Kerry and the rest of us look stupid. It would be just like him to tell some outlandish lie to Beth, who hung on his every word.

"Anyway, they're supposed to have the best pizza in town! It says so right there," said Beth, pointing to the sign above the cash register. Then she looked embarrassed, remembering that I wouldn't be eating any. "Oh, I'm sorry, Rissa," she quickly apologized. "But don't worry. We mentioned your allergy to the manager and he said there's lots of stuff you can order that doesn't have tomato."

I picked up a menu, trying to find the "lots of stuff" Beth had mentioned. I found fried chicken and pasta Alfredo, neither of which I particularly liked. Maybe I would just go over to the candy machine and get a handful of Skittles for dinner, I thought. As I was picturing all my guests gathered around, urging me to eat something more than candy so I wouldn't starve to death and scolding Beth for choosing to have the party at Dino's, the people we'd invited started showing up.

When Angel and Kerry came through the door together, the first thing I noticed about them was their hair. Even though the light was dim, I could see that they'd gotten blondish streaks just like Beth's. My first thought was that they were copycats. But deep down, I felt a pang of longing, and at that moment, I would have given *anything* to trade places with either one of them — just for a minute — to experience what it was like to have long, bouncy hair with shiny blond streaks.

Unfortunately, my hair would never look like theirs for two reasons:

★ 1. I could never get the money or permission to get a high-light job.

★ 2. The results could be disastrous.

Unlike my friends, I do not have normal hair. It is a mass of tangled curls that absolutely refuses to grow past my shoulders. Mom says my "problem" hair is a genetic thing, and I should "never, ever put harsh chemicals (like high-light solution) on it." Seeing as how I live in terror that someday my hair might stop growing altogether, I don't question her judgment.

"You like?" The girls shook their hair at me.

"Pretty!" I said, quickly turning my attention to the presents they were carrying. Was it too much to hope that someone had gotten me the miracle hair-growing formula I'd seen advertised on TV?

Yes, as it turned out, it was.

As was often the case at birthday parties, my idea about what might be in the packages was more imaginative (and expensive) than what was actually there. I ended up with some CDs, a couple of necklaces, a bottle of bath oil, and this little plastic troll doll that I guess Jayne Littleton thought was a gnome because she said it was for my gnome collection. All in all, it was kind of a disappointing haul.

Meanwhile, Beth was oohing and aahing with delight over the gifts she'd received. As I watched her hugging the other girls and thanking them for the perfect presents, I got a funny feeling in my stomach. And I think it was at that moment I first realized the horrible truth. Angel, Kerry, and Jayne understood Beth in a way I didn't, and none of them understood me at all. As this was running through my mind, I had to turn away from the hugging scene because my eyes were starting to water.

"Say cheese, Rissa!" My mother snapped my picture.

After my mom and Beth's mom took more pictures and finished throwing all of the wrapping paper in a big black garbage bag, it was time to order lunch. Everyone except me wanted pizza, naturally. When I gave the waitress my fried chicken order, she winked at my mother and said, "There always has to be one who's different, huh?" making me blush.

As I waited for the food to come, I stayed pretty quiet while everyone else discussed new clothes and what boys in our class they thought were "hot." I pretended to be interested, and smiled a lot — so much that my face started to ache — but all the time, I kept thinking, "They don't get me and I don't get them." The idea was stuck in my head and I couldn't get it out. I looked over at my mom, who was busy writing down the recipe for Mrs. White's artichoke dip, and I wished the party would hurry up and end.

Then suddenly, everybody around me stopped talking, and I saw Jayne Littleton elbow Beth.

"Look who just walked in," someone else said. I followed Beth's gaze, expecting to find some "hot" boy from our school. But it wasn't anyone like that. It was Brian Bailey, one of the nerdiest kids in our fifth grade class, who couldn't have picked a worse time to come to Dino's Pizzeria with his mother and grandfather.

"Hey, Rissa," Kerry announced shrilly. "Here comes your knight in shining armor."

"Shut UP" was all I could manage to say. Brian is the kind of kid everyone makes fun of. He's overweight, terrible at sports, and tends to sweat a lot. You know the type.

"Go over there and say hi," Angel said, giggling.

"No!"

Everyone had been giving me grief about Brian ever since fourth grade when he helped me get to the nurse's office after I sprained my ankle on the playground. I suppose for most people, walking down the hall with Brian Bailey would be one of the most humiliating moments of their lives. But this is the thing: Brian Bailey was really kind of helpful that day, saying things to try to make me laugh so I'd forget about how much pain I was in. I remember thinking, "People are unfair to poor old Brian. He's a really funny guy." I realize now that back then when I was in fourth grade, it would have been a good opportunity for me to "dare to be different" and say, "Hey, that Brian Bailey isn't such a bad kid." But I was only nine. What did I know about good opportunities?

Anyway, a couple of months after he rescued me on the playground, I saw Brian and his mother at the Salvation Army. Mom and I were there dropping off a load of Beth's hand-me-downs that I'd outgrown, and while Mom was getting her receipt, I noticed Brian and Mrs. Bailey standing over by the racks of winter coats. When I saw them looking through the jackets, I got this big old lump in my throat. I mean, it's bad enough to have to wear hand-me-downs from your best friend, but I could think of nothing worse than having to buy a coat for yourself that some *stranger* had once worn. Brian eventually noticed me staring at him, and instead of blushing with shame, like I would have done, he just gave me this big smile and waved. Now, I'm not saying I *like* Brian or anything, but I do have to admit he's a decent person. Secretly, I hope he grows up to be a famous scientist or multimillionaire, just so all the people in my class who made fun of him will be terribly jealous.

"I dare you to go over to him and invite him to sit with us," said Angel, who was always egging people on to do stuff they didn't want to do. I could feel my face getting hot. If I followed through with the dare, poor Brian would probably take me seriously and he *would* come over and join the party, not realizing the joke was on him. The last thing

I wanted to do was make him feel stupid in front of his mother and his grandfather.

"Do it! Do it!" the other girls started to chant. I waited for Beth, my supposed best friend, to tell everyone to cut it out, but she was screeching along with the rest of the girls and refused to look me in the eye.

Suddenly, all the pity I felt for Brian Bailey and mostly for myself went swirling around in my head, making me dizzy. It became very clear to me that I did not belong at this party. I did not belong with this group.

So I did it. I left the herd.

"You guys are a bunch of jerks," I told them. I must have spoken too loudly, because there was a sudden hush. Angel's eyes burned with anger. Beth looked shocked. So did the other girls. As I got up from my chair, my mother shot me a warning glance, which meant "Sit down this minute." But I did NOT sit down. There was nothing for me to do but head for the bathroom.

Now if I'd been thinking straighter, I might have realized that insulting every girl I knew right before the new school year started might not have been the smartest move in the world. But at the moment, I was all caught up in how different I was from them and how I needed to escape.

For a long, long time, I sat inside a locked stall with a string of toilet paper wrapped around my fist. I used the toilet paper to wipe my tears, which sprang to my eyes every time I thought about how mean everyone was being to me on my birthday, when they should have been acting *extra* nice. I hoped they felt ashamed. I hoped they wished I was back at the table. I expected one of them to come any second to sheepishly knock at my stall door, begging forgiveness.

When it appeared that nobody was going to show up, I had another thought. What if the girls didn't *realize* how mean they'd been to me? What if they just shrugged their shoulders when I left, instead of feeling ashamed? My tears dried up and I started to sweat, picturing the party going on full blast without me. I sort of wanted to go back inside the restaurant, but I couldn't think how to do it without looking like a fool and having everyone stare at me and poke each other under the table.

It was getting very uncomfortable, sitting on the toilet seat for so long. My thighs were starting to feel numb. There wasn't much to do except look at the graffiti on the door. DIANE + TAD, I read. ELIZABETH & RICHARD 4-EVER. M.C. IS A GREAT KISSER. Then I noticed a message written in really tiny letters near the bottom of the door. AMBER T. IS A TRAITOR! When I saw those words, it was like the writer was right there with me, knowing what it felt like to have your feelings hurt by a friend. *What had Amber T. done that was so terrible?* I wondered. Had she embarrassed her friend during a pizza party? Had she ditched her at the mall? And what had happened to the girl who wrote the graffiti? Did she forget all about Amber T. and go on to do wonderful things, or did her anger fester inside her and turn her insane?

As I wondered about the answers to these questions, more time passed. The bathroom was eerily quiet. I'd stopped expecting anyone to come beg for my forgiveness, but it seemed odd to me that none of my guests had needed to visit the bathroom for other reasons. Sooner or later, at least *one* of them would have to show up, I figured. I longed to wash my face, but I didn't want to go outside the stall, fearing that the moment I did, one of my guests would come into the bathroom and see me. Worse yet, I might run into Mrs. White, who has a way of giving you the critical eye whether or not you've done anything wrong.

Then the bathroom door *did* open, and I heard the familiar *click, click, click* of my mother's high-heeled sandals.

"Rissa, are you still in here?" Her voice echoed. I sniffed just loudly enough to signal where I was. "The food's here. You're missing your party."

"I know." Even though my mother was sitting right there at the table when the girls were chanting at me, I was pretty sure she was clueless about what was really going on. She and Mrs. White were in their own little world.

"If you are going to stay in here, that's your decision, but I think it's very rude behavior. Remember that this is Bethany's party, too. Mrs. White is *not* pleased."

Who cares? I thought angrily. You'd think my mother would be more concerned about what was going on with me than what other people, namely Mrs. White, thought.

"I don't want to come back," I said.

"Well, I can't bring your food into the bathroom, if that's what you're thinking. That stall is full of germs."

"I'm not hungry," I said. Of course I realized that I couldn't stay in the bathroom stall for the rest of my life, although it did seem to be a better alternative than facing a table full of girls who probably were as mad at me as I was at them. I pictured my chicken and mashed potatoes getting cold on my plate, a reminder that I was not a pizza eater. I was not like everyone else.

"You could at least have the courtesy to come out and look at the cake Mrs. White brought for you and Beth."

"You could take a picture of it," I suggested, remembering how I wanted to help pick out the cake, but Mom let Mrs. White be in charge of it. I thought of other times when my mother had taken Mrs. White's side instead of sticking up for what I wanted. There was the whole hand-me-down-clothes thing, of course, with Mom acting so grateful to Mrs. White for Beth's old clothes when she *knew* I didn't want them. I mean, sure, money was a little tight at our house with Mary Ann in college and all, but it wasn't *that* tight. Even though my father wasn't the president of a bank like Mr. White was, he made a pretty good salary working for our local TV station, selling commercial airtime to local businesses. Besides, I didn't have to wear *expensive* clothes. I didn't have to shop at the small pricey shops at the mall or go on regular sprees in Chicago like Beth did. A lot of kids I knew shopped the sales at regular department stores. That would have been just fine with me. Anything new would have been better than old pants, skirts, and sweater sets, no matter how "high quality" they were.

I stared at my mother's painted toenails under the door of the stall. In her mind, I was just acting like a brat. She didn't understand my feelings any more than my friends did. It was so unfair!

Then, after a few seconds of silence, her feet disappeared and she *click, click, click*ed out of the bathroom.

When I grow up and have a daughter, I'll be sensitive to her feelings, I thought. *And I won't let myself be pushed around by people like Mrs. White, either.* But even as I was thinking that, something was nudging at my conscience, and I knew, in the past, I *had* let myself get pushed around sometimes. I went to the mall with my friends even when I didn't want to go. I wore Beth's clothes even though I hated them, and I went ahead and agreed to have this birthday party at Dino's instead of just flat-out refusing. Well, those days were over, I vowed. The only problem was that I couldn't think of a graceful way to leave the bathroom and let everyone know it.

CHAPTER 5

HOME AND A NEW GNOME

When my mom returned to the bathroom to announce that all of the guests had gone home, I could tell she was upset with me. She didn't say a word as she helped me pack up my presents, and she was still silent on the way home.

"I think you should go upstairs and start writing thank-you notes," she said crisply as soon as we stepped into the house.

So that's exactly what I did. It didn't bother me to be sent to my room. I wanted to be alone. I yanked open my desk drawer and pulled out the note cards my grandmother had sent as part of my birthday present.

"*Dear Jayne,*" I wrote on the first card. "*Thank you for the troll doll. It looks a lot like you. Yours truly, Rissa Bartholomew.*" I knew I'd never send that note, but it felt good to write it. Next I wrote to Angel, thanking her for bath oil that smelled like "dish soap." While I wrote nasty letters, Mom, who has her own way of blowing off steam, was downstairs furiously cleaning. I could hear her vacuuming the living room. Then I heard her dusting the keys of the piano no one ever plays. I knew that she'd be in a better mood by the time she was finished, and I was right. A few minutes later, she knocked on my door.

"Let's not be mad at each other anymore, okay?" she said. "After all, it *is* your birthday." It wasn't exactly an apology, but it was close enough.

The house was absolutely spotless by the time my father and Mary Ann got home from the TV station. My sister — who was still trying to figure out what to do with her life — was working as his assistant that summer, but by now, she'd pretty much figured out that she wasn't cut out to be a salesperson.

"Can I open my family presents?" I asked my mom, eyeing the enormous box Dad had set down in the living room.

"Since we're all here, I think that would be all right," she said. For the first time that day, she smiled at me. It was kind of a tight-lipped smile, but I could tell she was softening.

"Here, open mine first." Mary Ann shoved a soft package wrapped in tissue paper at me.

I tore off the wrap in a hurry and found a T-shirt with DINO'S PIZZERIA written on the back.

"A little something to remember your eleventh birthday party," she said cheerfully. Obviously, she hadn't heard the news that the party was not exactly a huge success.

"Go ahead and open Dad's gift," Mom said eagerly.

I took my time with that present, trying to keep the suspense going as long as possible. I knew I was driving my mother nuts.

"You don't have to fold the wrapping paper. Just open the box," she said. Very slowly, I opened the box and immediately felt a rush of love for my dad. If the girls at my party were clueless about what I wanted, he wasn't.

In case you're wondering, my dad didn't get me a computer or a TV or anything like that. My parents don't spend that kind of money on birthdays. But he did get something he knew I really wanted. It was a gnome lawn ornament that I'd seen at the Rabbit Hole gift shop.

Okay, I know you're probably thinking: What does an eleven-year-old want a lawn ornament for? But I've had this thing about gnomes (NOT trolls, in case you're reading this, Jayne Littleton!) ever since I was a little kid. I think it was my grandma — the same one who gave me note cards this year — who got me my first gnome, and I've been collecting them ever since. My gnomes are like people to me. Just by looking at their faces, I can tell what their personalities are like and what they're feeling on the inside. Pip, my little wooden one from Germany, is the cool one, who's really laid-back. Timothy, who has hair hanging over his eyes, is really shy. Nicholas (who doubles as a Christmas tree ornament during the holiday season) always looks on the bright side of things.

I studied the face of the newest member of my gnome family. His forehead was wrinkled in concentration. He was peering straight ahead with these piercing eyes that seemed to look right through you. He didn't exactly look scary; it was more like he was noticing something few people could see. His name would be Nelson, I decided. Nelson, the wise old gnome. He could stand right at the foot of my bed and be my guard during the night.

"I love him!" I told my dad.

"I thought you were going to get her a beanbag chair," said Mom.

"I thought Rissa would like this better," Dad replied.

As is the tradition for all of our birthdays, Dad (who fantasizes about being a famous gourmet chef) cooked us dinner that night. He put steaks out on the grill and made that pineapple salad with marshmallows and coconut that I like so much. After the cookout, when I was feeling all full and a little sleepy, I could almost forget how badly most of the day had gone. All in all, things were going okay until Mom cleared her throat and made her announcement.

"Rissa, there's one more present for you." She paused

dramatically and exchanged a knowing glance with Dad. Dad smiled. Mary Ann shrugged her shoulders at me like she didn't know what was going on. Maybe this year my parents decided that they *would* get me something big for my birthday. A computer? A wide-screen TV for my room? My heart started beating faster.

"What is it?" I asked excitedly.

Mom took a deep breath. "I've decided to let you take ballet lessons this fall with Beth."

My heart leaped, but not in a good way. I didn't know what to say, but I was thinking, *BALLET LESSONS!?!?!?* She had to be kidding.

There was a long, awkward silence while I tried to think of a response. I hadn't thought about ballet lessons since second grade when I was jealous of Beth's pink leotard. But ballet had always been Beth's thing and I had no intention of being a copycat or going to a beginning dance class when Beth was already in an advanced class, wearing toe shoes and everything.

"That's really nice," I eventually said, forcing my mouth into a smile. "But I don't think I'd be very good at ballet."

Mom's face fell. Dad looked disappointed, too. Then I really felt crummy for making them feel so bad.

"It's just that I was hoping to do something different this year," I added.

"What?" my parents asked expectantly.

I had to do some quick thinking, which, luckily, I'm good at.

"Well, um, I've always kind of wanted to play the violin. It's sort of been this dream of mine."

Don't ask me why I said that. I don't really know why playing the violin popped into my mind. Maybe it was because Mary Ann and I had just seen the video *Music of the Heart*. You know, that movie where that music teacher starts a school orchestra in the ghetto. I remember thinking that being a member of the school orchestra wouldn't be so bad if you got a chance to play in Carnegie Hall with a bunch of really famous musicians like the kids in the movie did.

"Funny," said Dad, "it wasn't your dream to play violin last year when your school started its orchestra program. As I recall, you said that only 'geeky' kids played instruments."

"Well, maybe it hasn't always been my dream," I had to admit.

"Do you *really* want to take violin lessons?" Dad asked suspiciously.

"Yes, I do." I crossed my arms over my chest and tipped my chair back just far enough to make Mom hold her breath.

"You know what I think this is?" My father also crossed his arms, but he had the good sense not to try leaning back in his chair. "I think this is Rissa Bartholomew's declaration of independence."

My "declaration of independence." I liked the way that sounded.

"I think it's too late to sign up for orchestra, and private music lessons could be very expensive," said Mom.

"How about this?" said Dad, putting his arm around Mom. "You try out violin lessons for three months, and if you practice every day and still have an interest in it after that, you may continue for as long as you like."

"Okay," I agreed.

Mom shot Dad one of her glares, which meant "This is something we should have talked about in private." I knew there would be more discussions about violin lessons after I'd gone to bed, but I was pretty confident that in the end, my dad would have the last word.

CHAPTER 6

FRIENDSHIP IS NO MOLEHILL

The next morning I woke up to a man peering over my bed. It was Nelson the Gnome. For a second I thought he was talking to me or I was dreaming he was talking to me. Then I realized that the voice I heard was coming from Mary Ann's bedroom next door.

"And at the pizza place, she spent most of the time in the bathroom, sulking," my mother was saying. Mary Ann said something back, but her voice was muffled.

I pulled my covers over my head, wishing I could make myself disappear. The last thing I wanted to think about was what had happened at my party, and I couldn't believe that my mom was telling Mary Ann all about it.

"Rissa, are you awake?" Now Mom was in the hall. "Get up, I need to talk to you."

"What?" I kept my eyes closed.

"Mrs. White just called. She tells me that Beth doesn't want to walk with you to school on Monday."

Buried under my comforter, I felt something sour-tasting lurch up in my throat. Leave it to Mrs. White to report the latest gossip about her daughter.

Finding out Beth didn't want to be with me on our very first day of middle school made me feel more scared and lonely than I wanted to admit. We'd *always* gone to school together, even before Jayne, Kerry, and Angel were in the picture.

I remembered our first day of kindergarten and how our mothers had made such a fuss, taking loads of pictures, reminding us of rules we should follow, and trailing behind us as we walked to school to make sure that we arrived safely. Even though we were being watched and there was no chance we'd lose our way, Beth and I tightly held hands, nervous about meeting our teacher and our classmates.

"I don't want to walk to school with Beth, either," I said, making my voice sound more certain than I felt.

"Rissa, I think we need to talk about this."

"For goodness' sake," Mary Ann interrupted. "Rissa's old enough to make her own decisions. Let her walk with whomever she wants." I peeked out from under my covers and found Mary Ann standing next to my mother with her arms crossed. "Let her walk alone if she wants. . . . *I* walked to school alone and nobody seemed too concerned about *me*."

Both Mom and I stared at my sister. We were used to her whining, but we were not used to her doing it for my benefit.

"You were mature for your age," my mother said. "Go back to your room and finish packing."

In two days, Mary Ann would be going back to University of Illinois, which was only about thirty miles away, but sometimes everyone acted like it was on the other side of the world. This year, she was going to be truly independent. Instead of living in the dorm, she was moving into an apartment with some of her friends.

I wished I could be Mary Ann.

"Rissa, I think it is very unwise of you to start off the year on the wrong foot," Mom said, directing her attention back to me despite the fact my sister did *not* go back to her room as told. "Is some argument you may have had with Beth important enough to jeopardize your whole friendship?"

"Really, Mother, sometimes you make a mountain out of a molehill," Mary Ann interrupted again.

"Friendship is no molehill," my mother replied firmly. "And it seems to me that if anyone is making mountains out of molehills, it's your sister, who has been friends with

Beth *forever*, and is now letting some silly squabble come between them."

"Could we talk more about this later in private?" I begged, hoping my mother would cool down and forget the whole thing.

"I think we need to get this straightened out right now." Mom stepped inside my room and shut the door. "You've walked to school with Beth — Bethany — nearly every day for the past five years. And what's going to happen when the weather turns cold? We have the car pool all worked out."

"*Car pool???* Rissa gets *rides* to middle school?" Mary Ann's voice carried through the closed door. Clearly, she was more into this conversation than I was. "When I was Rissa's age, I *walked* when the weather was bad. I walked when it rained. I walked when it snowed. I walked during that ice storm when school was *canceled* and you forgot to check the listings before sending me out in the cold."

Mom ignored Mary Ann and stepped closer to my bed.

"Maybe we *should* wait and discuss this in private," she said. "I'll be downstairs when you're ready."

After my mother had left, I got out of bed and put on the same shorts and T-shirt I'd worn to my party. When I was putting on my sneakers, Mary Ann knocked on the wall separating our rooms.

"Are you okay in there?" she asked.

"Yeah."

"Why don't you come in here and keep me company while I pack?"

Invitations to do something with Mary Ann didn't come very often and I suspected she wanted to grill me about my birthday party and why I didn't want to walk to school with Beth. I made my way around piles of junk strewn all over the hallway and stepped into her room, which looked pretty much like a place hit by a tornado.

Empty bags littered her floor. Boxes marked SALVATION ARMY were overflowing with worn-out pants and T-shirts. Unlike Beth, Mary Ann knew better than to hand down her old clothes to people she knew. She delivered them directly to the Salvation Army without letting Mom see what she was giving away. Otherwise, you can just bet my mother would save the clothes for me, patching up holes and sewing split seams to try to squeeze out a few extra years of wear. I could just see Mom carrying armloads of musty, dusty, patched-up clothes from the attic, saying, "Never mind if it's been ten years since Mary Ann wore these. They're still good as new."

"You don't want any of those, do you?" Mary Ann asked as she saw me eyeing the clothes in the Salvation Army box.

I shook my head and turned my eyes to her bed. Seeing the open suitcase there made me a little sad, I have to admit. In a weird sort of way, I was kind of sorry that my sister would be leaving so soon. Not only was it a sign that summer was coming to an end, but the truth was that I was going to miss Mary Ann. We didn't always get along and she still tended to be a drama queen at times, but when she was around, my mother had someone else to argue with besides me.

"What's going on between you and Bethany White?"

"Her name's Beth, not Bethany."

Mary Ann shrugged. "Mom said she wants to be called Bethany now. Anyway, what did you two have a fight about?"

"Nothing. We're just not so close anymore."

I'm sure Mary Ann expected me to go on and explain things more fully, but what was there to say? The truth was that knowing Beth didn't want to walk with me hurt my feelings more than I could have explained. I wasn't even sure if I could find my homeroom without Beth. Though she had her faults, Beth was very good with directions. I was not. I didn't realize until then that being independent might also mean being alone.

"So, are you scared about starting middle school?" Mary Ann asked.

I didn't answer right away. Why would she suddenly ask me that? Maybe my mother had asked her to pump me for information. I guess I'd been dropping some hints that I was not exactly thrilled about the idea of starting the new year, unlike Beth, who'd been making plans for middle school since last May.

"Why should I be scared?" I asked.

"I don't know, but if you *were* scared, you shouldn't be. In some ways, middle school is a lot better than grade school."

"I guess it won't be that bad."

"Do you know anything about your teachers?"

"I got Mrs. Lucas for homeroom."

"You're kidding! Mrs. Lucas?" Mary Ann said, smiling. "I had her when I was in sixth grade. Actually, she was a really good teacher."

This information came as a surprise to me. Not just that Mary Ann had Mrs. Lucas for a teacher, but the fact that she liked her. According to Kerry's brother (who, of course, might not be the most reliable source), Mrs. Lucas was one of the strictest teachers in middle school. Nobody, not even eighth graders, tangled with her.

"I wouldn't know the difference between a direct object and a predicate nominative if it wasn't for Mrs. Lucas," Mary Ann added.

"Really?" I said, pretending that I knew what she was

talking about. Then Mary Ann told me a story about what happened the time Mrs. Lucas caught some poor sixth grader cheating. If she was trying to comfort me, she was doing a pretty bad job.

"Anyway, in middle school you'll have a chance to meet new kids and make new friends," she reminded me.

"Did you have a lot of friends?" I asked.

"I had a couple of good ones. That's all you need."

"Were you part of a group?"

"Yeah. Everyone pretty much is in middle school."

"Weren't there any kids who hung out by themselves?" I asked.

"Do you mean outcasts?" Mary Ann gave me a funny look. "I guess there were a few of them. I remember this one guy who was really good at chess and wore a suit to school every day. He kind of marched to the beat of a different drummer. Everyone thought he was kind of strange."

Obviously, Mary Ann's generation hadn't gotten the "It's okay not to follow the herd" lectures at school.

"I've kind of left my group of friends," I confessed. "I guess I'm on my own now."

Mary Ann seemed surprised by the news. I guess Mom hadn't told her *all* the details about the party. "So, the fight you had at the restaurant wasn't just with Beth?"

I shook my head.

"You told *all* your friends off?"

I nodded.

"Why would you do a thing like that right before school starts?"

Mary Ann waited for an answer, but I didn't have one. I was beginning to think I'd made a horrible mistake.

CHAPTER 7

THE LESSON

Mom and I never had our "private" talk about me not walking to school with Beth, but I was pretty sure she and my sister had some discussions about it. There was some heavy-duty whispering going on when they thought I was asleep, and I thought I heard my name and phrases like "make her own decisions" mentioned a couple of times.

Then Mom got all distracted with Mary Ann going back to school. There were discussions about what Mary Ann should and shouldn't take. There were conversations about how much stuff would fit in the car and what should or should not be delivered by mail. Mom shed some tears the day Mary Ann left. I kept mine inside as I noticed how the house felt emptier all of a sudden.

The closer the first day of school came, the more nervous I got. At the same time I was having some doubts about leaving "the herd," I was also having some doubts about the whole violin lesson thing. It was fun imagining myself as a violinist, and I loved the violin that Dad rented for me from the music shop. But my first lesson, which occurred a few days before my first day of school, was not exactly what I hoped.

Although I liked my violin teacher's name, Lee G. Keesly (fun to say, isn't it?), I wasn't sure what to make of the man himself. When I first saw him, I had this weird feeling that I knew him from somewhere. He was pretty old and kind of hunched over, and he had a little potbelly. Then it occurred to me that he looked sort of like my gnome, Pip, and that made me warm up to Mr. Keesly a little. So did the fact he had a pet, a Chihuahua dog named Sparky, who was about as ancient as his owner.

I was hoping to at least learn how to play "Jingle Bells" during my first lesson. But Mr. Keesly was in no hurry to teach me any song at all. In fact, he seemed more interested in my singing voice than my new violin.

He was thrilled to learn that I already knew the musical scale (everyone learns it in the second grade) and he made me sing "do, re, mi" while he played along with me on the piano. He plunked the keys so hard that poor Sparky, who had been resting peacefully under the piano, jerked up his head in alarm.

"Oh my, you're an alto, aren't you?" Mr. Keesly commented when he noticed that my "do" sounded pretty much like my "la." Then he made me start all over again, singing the scale, starting out on a lower note. I can't tell you how awkward it was to sing in Mr. Keesly's living room under the watchful eye of Sparky with my dad in the background coughing to cover up the fact that he was laughing at me.

"Well, I think that's enough singing for today," Mr. Keesly said briskly when I was done with that second round of "do, re, mi." "Let's have her practice that at home, Father," he said to Dad.

Anyway, after the exhausting and embarrassing singing part of the lesson was over, I figured it was time to open my violin case, but Mr. Keesly had other plans. He put this pencil across the black keys of the piano and demonstrated the correct way to pick up a violin bow.

When I got home, Mom, who'd finally accepted the idea that I was not going to become a ballerina like Beth, made me show her what I learned. I felt pretty dumb doing my bow exercises and demonstrating the proper way to hold a violin, but she seemed pleased enough. I think Dad and I were in agreement that it wasn't necessary for me to demonstrate how I could sing the musical scale.

CHAPTER 8

NEW-BEGINNING BLUES

Usually I hate rainy mornings, but on the first day of school, when I woke up to thunder and lightning, I felt this big wave of relief. I knew that since it was raining, my dad would give me a ride to school, and I didn't have to worry about walking alone.

I tried to think comforting thoughts as I prepared myself for the day. I had new school supplies (at least Mrs. White didn't hand those down!), and by 3:30, I'd be back home doing whatever I wanted.

But after breakfast, when it was almost time to leave the house, the butterflies in the pit of my stomach, which had kept me awake late into the night, came back. I was hoping Dad and I could make a clean break before Mom could say anything about school that would make me more nervous than I already was, but she caught us before we got out the door.

"Honestly, Rissa," she said. "It's pouring rain out and you aren't even wearing a raincoat."

What raincoat? Surely my mother wasn't thinking of the hand-me-down yellow slicker Beth had passed down to me ages ago.

"I don't have a raincoat that fits," I told her.

"What do you mean you don't have one?"

"All my coats and jackets, except my winter one, are too small."

My mother frowned.

"What about that red Windbreaker that Beth gave you last spring?"

"Hm, I don't remember it."

Of course I did, and I knew exactly where it was, hanging in the very back of the coat closet. But my mother didn't need to know this.

"Well, at least take an umbrella," she sighed.

"That's okay." Even I knew that starting middle school with an umbrella dangling from my wrist was a highly uncool thing to do. "I'll just be running from the car to the building."

"Fine. Get drenched." My mother threw up her hands in surrender and turned away as Dad and I made a mad dash for the car.

The windshield wipers creaked mournfully as we passed the Whites' house, and I noticed their car was missing from the driveway. Mrs. White was probably giving Beth a ride to school. I wondered if she was going to pick up Jayne, Kerry, and Angel on her way.

"Well, how does it feel to be a sixth grader?" Dad asked.

"About the same as being a fifth grader, I guess," I said.

From the parking lot of the middle school, the building itself looked very dark and dreary. Maybe it was because of the rain or maybe not. Even when the sun was shining, it loomed huge and unfriendly on the edge of the city's downtown area.

I watched other kids getting out of cars. Some looked eager. A few looked a little scared. Others were pretending to be bored. Most of them looked like they were wearing new clothes.

Slowly, I pushed my car door open. It seemed heavier than usual.

"Have a good day," said Dad.

I'd settle for not getting lost.

On the way to the building, I did get drenched as my mother predicted, but the good thing was that I didn't have to worry about finding my classroom. There was a guide stationed just inside the door, and she directed me where to go on the second floor.

As soon as I finished climbing the stairs, I saw Beth and

the rest of the group at the end of the hallway, huddled around the doorway of my homeroom. I expected Beth to be wearing her new birthday outfit that she wore to the party, but she was wearing a different one, a short, pale yellow, pleated skirt and cotton sweater that matched exactly. All of the other girls were wearing skirts, too. They were acting like copycats again, but it didn't make me feel better to know that I wasn't following the crowd. Actually, I felt kind of uncomfortable, like I wasn't dressed up enough. And I didn't know if I should say hi to them or just leave them alone.

As I cautiously approached the crowd, not knowing what to expect, the girls stopped watching Kerry, who was telling a story and shaking rain out of her highlighted hair at the same time. Suddenly, all eyes were on me, or rather my shirt. I was wearing the Dino's Pizzeria one that Mary Ann gave me for my birthday. I know that may seem like a weird choice, given the fact I am not a big fan of Dino's, but it was something I had that never belonged to Beth. What can I say?

"Er, Rissa," Angel said, looking at the other girls. "You really need to wear a bra with that shirt if you plan to wear it in the rain."

I looked down at my shirt and realized what she meant.

"Not that there's all that much to see," Kerry added, causing the girls to break into giggles.

"Excuse me," I said hotly, covering my chest with my backpack. I shouldered my way through their little huddle and went into the room, hoping the girls would keep the news about my wet T-shirt to themselves.

CHAPTER 9

TABLE FOR TWO

I slunk into a seat at the back of the room, where I hoped my shirt, which I was trying to fan dry, would remain unnoticed. What I needed to do was look forward, not backward, I thought, trying to put my ex-friends out of my mind. The first day of school *could* be full of opportunities for meeting new people and making new friends.

Mrs. Lucas was sitting at her desk, and there were two other people in the classroom. One of them was Kyle Jacobs, the brain. We went to grade school together, and I knew I didn't have to worry about him staring at my chest. He didn't pay much attention to girls.

The other person in the room, who was standing at Mrs. Lucas's desk, was a girl I didn't know. She had two long braids, and I felt a pang of jealousy, seeing how far they went down her back. I stopped fanning my shirt and tugged a strand of my hair, a habit I'd had since I was little, when I still had hope it would grow past my shoulders.

"Vermont is a beautiful state. You must miss the mountains," Mrs. Lucas said to the girl.

I leaned forward in my desk and strained to hear more, wondering why someone from Vermont would move to Hickory Grove, Illinois. The girl must have felt me staring at her because she glanced my way. I smiled. She blinked and turned back to Mrs. Lucas, who said, "You may have a seat now, Violet."

Now that's *a name you don't hear every day,* I thought. I hoped Violet would come sit next to me, but she chose a seat on the other side of the room near a window.

I could tell just by looking at her that this new girl wasn't into trendy fashions the way my ex-friends were. She had her own personal style. Besides having the longest hair of any person I'd seen, she'd transformed a pair of perfectly ordinary denim overall shorts into something new and different by embroidering vines and leaves up the side seams. The effect was pretty cool, and I wondered if I could do something original like that to some of Beth's hand-me-downs. Maybe Violet could show me how.

I imagined this little scene with us sitting upstairs in my bedroom, busily sewing designs on some jeans.

I'd say, "Maybe you could spend the night so we could watch the Creature Feature together."

She would say, "Ooh, I *love* the Creature Feature."

And as simply as that, I'd have a new best friend.

When Violet took off her glasses to wipe them on her sleeve, I willed her to look over at me. But instead, she opened a thick book and began to read, completely ignoring everything around her. She sat perfectly still until the warning bell sounded, making both of us jerk in our seats.

Suddenly, there was a flurry of activity with students coming through the door and trying to find seats by their friends. Beth and Jayne sat down at desks in the middle of the room, making a point of ignoring me as they swept past. Some boys who played soccer at my old grade school sat down in the back of the room with me, but they didn't give me much more of a glance than Beth and Jayne did. They were too busy gazing at the two girls sitting in front of me, who looked like they belonged in high school and wore clothes that I was sure broke about every dress-code rule in the book.

Then Brian Bailey came into the room, making my heart leap as the memory of my birthday party came rushing back. He, of course, was the one student who noticed me. On his way to the front of the room, he stopped at my desk to ask how my summer was.

"It was all right," I told him, my eyes darting frantically

around the room to see if anyone I knew was watching us have a conversation. On the very first day of school, I didn't want to get pegged as the girl who hung out with the nerdy kid, and I was afraid Brian might mention seeing me at Dino's.

"Well, see you around," said Brian, catching on to the fact I didn't want to talk.

"Yeah, see you," I said. Then I noticed Brian's eyes, how trusting and honest they seemed, and I felt ashamed for brushing him off.

After glancing back over at Violet, who still had her nose buried in a book, I examined some of the other kids, wondering if any of them might be looking for a new friend. Hickory Grove Middle School drew its students from four different elementary schools, so most of the sixth graders were strangers to me. It was kind of disappointing to see that almost all of them seemed to have friends already. People were chatting away, catching up on one another's news.

"All right, we're going to get started now," Mrs. Lucas announced about one second after the final bell rang. Then she gave us a look, daring anyone to challenge her.

The talking stopped, and everyone sat straighter in their seats as roll call began. My name came right after Brian Bailey's. When Mrs. Lucas called it, I was surprised that she called me Rissa instead of Clarissa, like most teachers did on the first day. That was definitely a point in her favor. Then she asked me if I was related to Mary Ann.

"She's my sister," I said, kind of proud that Mrs. Lucas would remember Mary Ann. "She's in college now."

"Really?" Mrs. Lucas looked surprised. "Well, I hope you don't turn out to be as much of a chatterbox as she was."

There was some nervous laughter, but not from me. I was too shocked. Wasn't comparing a student to his/her sister a huge no-no?

I jumped to my sister's defense, saying, "Mary Ann doesn't have much time to chatter now that she's studying to be a doctor," realizing too late that Mrs. Lucas was just teasing me. Then I felt enormously stupid, making this huge announcement that my sister was going to be a doctor when the truth of the matter was that she had no clue what she wanted to be. Beth, who knew Mary Ann pretty well, probably thought I'd lost my mind.

After that humiliating moment, the rest of the morning was filled with the usual first day of school stuff. We had to write an essay about "Personal goals for our sixth grade year." Before I put down words on paper, I brainstormed a list in my head:

★ 1. I will find a whole new set of friends.

★ 2. I will not let people push me around.

★ 3. I will do something about my clothes problem.

★ 4. I will never tell another lie about a family member in front of the class.

I didn't think Mrs. Lucas would be too interested in any of this, so I ended up writing this really lame paper about how I hoped to improve my math skills.

When I was done with my essay, it was almost lunchtime, and I was getting hungry. I thought about the lunch bag in my locker, and wondered what my mother had packed for me. I wondered if the rest of the girls and I would trade stuff at lunch like we normally did in grade school. Beth always had homemade cookies or cupcakes.

Then it hit me.

I wouldn't be eating lunch with Beth. And that's when I started to panic. Where was I going to eat? I mean, I knew I'd go to the cafeteria with everyone else, but where would I sit? If middle school was anything like grade school, those people who were not members of a group had a definite disadvantage in the cafeteria. Images of Brian Bailey standing alone with his tray, pitifully searching for a table flashed through my mind. I couldn't bear the idea of me being in his shoes, having people feel sorry for me or smirk at me or put books on a chair so I knew a seat was saved. I wanted to be independent, not an outcast like him or that chess-boy-in-a-suit Mary Ann remembered from her middle school days.

As the minutes ticked away, I scanned the room, trying to find someone I knew who might let me eat lunch with them. If I was bolder and more kindhearted, I *might* have asked Brian, but I'd only been independent for a few days. I just wasn't that courageous yet. I studied every girl in the room, trying to match names from roll call with faces. I wished there were more kids from my old school, but besides Jayne and Beth (whose mother had called the principal to make sure we three were in the same class), there was just Brian, Kyle, and the soccer players, who sat in the back of the room with me.

My eyes landed on Violet, and my heart lifted a little. Even though we weren't exactly friends yet, we *had* made eye contact, and that counted for something. Besides, I was desperate.

When twelve o'clock finally rolled around and we were dismissed, I practically pounced on her in the hall.

"You want to eat together?" I asked in a friendly way, thinking she'd be flattered.

"Are you talking to me?" Violet looked over her shoulder.

"Yeah. Let's get to the cafeteria before all the tables are taken."

"I don't know." She took her time getting her lunch from her locker. "I was thinking about getting permission to go to the media center. I kind of like to read while I eat."

"There's no eating allowed in the media center," I insisted, although I wasn't sure if this was true. "I'll be quiet and let you read, okay?"

Violet didn't smile. She just stared at me. Then she started walking, and I followed, hoping she was headed in the direction of the cafeteria since I wasn't sure I remembered how to get there.

"What are you reading?" I asked her, hoping to distract her from the idea of eating alone. Maybe we liked the same kinds of books, I thought. Books would be something we could talk about over lunch.

"*The Knight with the Silver Sword.*" Violet pulled out the thick volume she'd been reading before class and showed me the cover.

There was a picture of a knight on a reared-up horse. In the knight's hand was an enormous sword.

"It's a fantasy that takes place during medieval times," Violet explained.

"Oh." Personally, I like the kind of books that take place in modern times about everyday kids going through dramatic crises, like discovering a dead body on a hiking trip or finding out they've been adopted. Have you read *The*

Face on the Milk Carton? That's a pretty good one, but I doubted if Violet had read it.

When Violet was done describing various characters from her book — warriors and damsels in distress and a few princes and princesses — she abruptly stopped talking. She seemed perfectly comfortable with the silence, but I was not. There were so many things I wanted to discuss about what was happening here and now, not a few hundred years ago. I longed to talk about Mrs. Lucas, for instance. Was she going to be as strict as everyone said she was? Would sixth grade be hard? I guess I could have asked Violet those questions, but suddenly I was feeling a little awkward. I thought they might be the wrong questions to ask.

"I really like your overalls. Did you embroider them yourself?" I asked.

Violet looked down at her pants legs as though she'd forgotten what she was wearing.

"My mother embroidered them."

So much for Violet and me working together to make our clothes new and different.

When we reached the cafeteria (moving at Violet's snail pace), most kids had already found tables and there weren't a whole lot of empty seats left. I glanced over to Beth's table, which still had a couple of seats open, and wondered who would sit there.

Meanwhile, Violet plopped down at the table everyone else had avoided. It was the one next to the cafeteria monitor, a woman with meaty arms, who wore an earring in her nose and had hair even shorter than mine. She was hunched over a paperback copy of *The Outsiders*, which happens to be another book I really like. It was pretty sad, I thought, that I might have more in common with the lunch lady than Violet.

By the time I'd settled down in my seat, Violet had laid her massive hardback book flat on the table, and was already pulling out a pie-shaped Tupperware from her lunch bag.

"What do you have there?" I asked, trying to make conversation.

"Cold pizza."

When I looked inside my own lunch bag, a lump rose in my throat. There was a peanut butter sandwich, tropical salad left over from my birthday dinner, and homemade chocolate chip cookies. My mother, who had been a total grouch all weekend, had packed my favorite lunch and had enclosed a note.

It said: HAVE A GREAT FIRST DAY!

CHAPTER 10

HOME ALONE

The house was empty when I got home from school. Dad was still at work and Mom was at the grocery store, according to the note she left on the kitchen table. I was glad I wouldn't have to answer any questions about school, but at the same time, I felt hungry for company. I had hardly talked to anyone all day, and I wasn't used to that.

After grabbing a couple of cookies, I went upstairs to visit with my gnomes, which has been part of my after-school routine ever since I was in kindergarten. I told them secrets, stuff I'd never mention to Mom or Dad or Mary Ann. And the best part was that they never scolded me or teased me or thought my problems were silly. Even when I couldn't find the right words to explain something, my gnomes understood what I was trying to say.

That afternoon, I told them how my first day at school

had felt like a horrible game of musical chairs with me always being the odd one out.

After lunch, we had traded rooms and met our math and science teacher, Mr. Jordan ("Call me Mr. J."). He turned out to be one of those young types who tries to be really hip and jokes around a lot with a few select kids and pretty much ignores the rest of the class.

We didn't have PE. It would start tomorrow. But we did get to go to our elective classes, and I'd chosen art for the first half of the year. It was held in a special room on the first floor, and instead of sitting at desks, we sat at tables, so it was like lunchtime all over again with me scurrying to get a seat next to Violet, who was also taking art. Another girl beat me there, though. I had no choice except to head for the chair next to Angel, and she gave me an icy stare, making sure that I knew I wasn't welcome.

I think that's when it really dawned on me that the gate separating me from my old friends had been shut and wouldn't open up again anytime soon. I guess in the back of my mind I thought that if I *wanted* to go back to them, I could. But that's *not* what I wanted, was it? Being independent was cool, right?

I looked at Nelson for reassurance, and I could almost hear him say, "Things will get better." Then Tim and

Nicholas and Pip and the others told me they'd always be my friends.

I appreciated my gnomes' support, but I had this sinking feeling that they might be my *only* friends for a while. Who would have thought that it would be so hard for a strong, independent-type person like me to find a *human* friend (not to mention a seat) on the first day of middle school? Where were the shy new kids, who were just waiting for someone like me to draw them out of their shells? Where were the other students who had left their old friends over the summer and were ready to make a fresh start? Why wasn't anyone noticing me?

Nelson (who was tending to sound like a fortune cookie sometimes) told me not to worry; new friends would come my way. But it was hard for me to believe him.

I dug into my backpack for the flyer we'd gotten at school that listed all the extracurricular activities and clubs that sixth graders could join. Joining a club would be a good way to meet kids, I figured. Unfortunately, all the clubs looked pretty boring except for girls' volleyball, and that wouldn't start until after Christmas.

Last year, Beth and Kerry had talked about trying out for the cheerleading squad and the rest of us said we'd go for it, too. We practiced doing cartwheels and jumps in Kerry's backyard. Kerry was good since she's taken gymnastics for so many years. Beth was pretty good, too. With all that ballet training, she could leap pretty high and she was the only one besides Kerry who could do the splits. The rest of us were average, I guess.

I stood in front of the mirror and practiced a couple of jumps. I looked like an idiot. There was no denying it. I was definitely not cheerleader material. In a way it was kind of a relief to know that Beth wouldn't be asking me to be her tryout partner now that we weren't best friends anymore, but another part of me felt like I would be missing out on something.

"If I'm not Beth's best friend anymore, who am I?" I asked myself. As I looked at my reflection in the mirror, the only answer I could come up with was that I was a girl who definitely needed a bra. There was nothing Nelson or any of my other gnomes could do to help me with that problem, but I thought I knew someone who could.

Mary Ann's phone was busy the first few times I tried to call her, but when I did get ahold of her, she seemed pleased to hear from me. She was anxious to tell me about how she'd fixed up her apartment. I listened as patiently as I could, wondering how I could turn the topic to me. Finally, I just had to interrupt when she started telling me about the bathroom curtains she'd just hung.

"I need you to do something for me," I said, then lowered my voice and told her what I needed. I must have kind of mumbled because she didn't understand what I said at first.

"What? A rock? Why do you need me to send you a rock?" she asked.

"Not a rock. A *bra*," I said a little louder. There was a minute of dead silence, then she started chuckling. *She could have been a little more sensitive,* I thought angrily. I was pretty fed up with people laughing at me.

"You want me to send you a BRA?" she asked between snorts.

"Yes, as fast as you can. Size small."

"Rissa," Mary Ann's voice took on a know-it-all tone, "I think that's something you need to get with Mom. Bra sizes aren't like shirt sizes. And it's really important that you get one that fits right."

"But I *can't* talk to Mom about it," I told her. I could just imagine what bra shopping would be like with my mom. First she'd call up Beth's mother to check if Beth had outgrown any of her bras, then she'd ask Beth's mother's advice on the whole matter. Then, if no used bras were available, she'd drag me to some old lady store to find me the cheapest, ugliest, most practical bra in the history of the world.

"Please, Mary Ann?" I begged. "I'll pay you back next

time I have some money. I promise." I'm usually not the type of person who resorts to begging, but this was a special case. There were a couple more minutes of silence while Mary Ann considered doing me the favor.

"Going shopping with Mom is pretty bad, isn't it?" she said, sighing.

"The worst."

And with that, Mary Ann agreed to help me out.

Once I'd settled the bra dilemma, I was inspired to do some planning about the rest of my wardrobe. I wanted to wear things that made me stand out and be more visible to those people who might be searching for a new friend.

I remembered the embroidered overalls that the new girl, Violet Hayes, wore. I wasn't in the mood to try anything as complicated as embroidering, but there might be another way I could perk up my clothes and turn them into something *no one* could recognize as Beth White's old things.

I went to my closet and pulled out my most recently delivered box of hand-me-downs. There was a pair of jeans that I sort of liked, and there was a turtleneck sweater that fit really well. There was also a denim skirt that would have been really cute if it wasn't bright pink, Beth's trademark color; that went great with her highlighted blond hair but looked pretty hideous on a person like me. Besides being curly and short, my hair is reddish brown.

I remembered how Mary Ann had tie-dyed some of her old T-shirts back when she was in high school, so I searched the linen closet for the dye she had used. It was gone, but there was a bottle half full of black dye that my mother had used to make a costume for me when our fourth grade class was doing a pageant on weather. (I had been a little black thundercloud. Beth was the rainbow after the storm.)

I read the instructions printed on the back of the dye. They seemed simple enough. There were several steps involved, but nothing I couldn't handle.

By now I was feeling a lot less lonely, and I didn't mind so much that my mother wasn't home. I wasn't sure if she'd approve of what I was doing, but she'd *surely* be impressed with the results. Mom herself was really into doing crafts, especially ones involving fabric. She'd be proud to see me create something of my own as long as I didn't make too much of a mess.

CHAPTER 11

I BOLDLY PERSEVERE

The next morning, Mom was quieter than usual when she fixed my breakfast. After giving me my plate of scrambled eggs, she sat down at the table.

"Do you notice anything different about me?" she asked.

Was this a trick question? I looked at her, trying to find something to compliment. She was wearing a gray shirt and shorts. Her hair looked the same as it always did, and she wasn't wearing any makeup.

"Um, is that a new shirt?"

"Good guess. Actually, it's not new. It *used* to be my good white blouse, but something seems to have happened to it when I ran it through the washer this morning."

"Oh."

"I couldn't figure out what happened, but then I noticed some clothes hanging over the sweater rack. Some very black, rather damp clothes that looked like they might belong to you."

I was going to wait to tell my mother about my dyeing project. Who would have thought she'd be doing laundry at the crack of dawn?

"I just wanted to make some of Beth's old clothes look more like *me*," I confessed.

My mother's eyes went wide with alarm. "You're not going Goth, are you?" She put her hand over her heart.

I remembered how worried she and Aunt Katrina were when my sixteen-year-old cousin, Tiffany, went through her Goth phase, wearing black clothes, black eyeliner, and black lipstick.

"I'm not going Goth," I assured my mother.

She breathed a sigh of relief.

"Well then, what were you thinking? Those were *beautiful* clothes." Mom shook her head like she didn't know what to do with me. "I would have given anything to have clothes like that when I was a girl. I had to *make* my own."

I knew this already. I'd heard the story a thousand times, about how my mother's parents didn't have much money and how Mom joined a 4-H club so she could learn how to sew. Her biggest accomplishment was making a fully lined wool suit that won her a blue ribbon at the state fair. It still hung in the attic.

One of my earliest memories was of Mom sitting at the sewing machine with scraps of fabric all around her, and her sketchbook lying open to the drawing of whatever she was making. I had to admit that besides being good at sewing, my mom was also pretty original when it came to fashion design. Some of her ideas were a little over the top (like the "kitty" sweatshirt with ears on the hood), but some of her stuff was pretty cool. Now and then (especially when I got a new box of hand-me-downs), I felt a pang of regret that Mom had given up sewing, especially since it was partly my fault.

"Sorry, Mom," I said.

"Does this have anything to do with your being angry with Beth? Did you deliberately ruin your clothes because they belonged to her?" Mom's mind was racing pretty fast for so early in the morning.

"Of course not," I told her, taking my plate to the sink.

Thankfully, that was the moment my father chose to come into the kitchen, jangling his keys.

"If you're ready to go, I could take you to school again this morning," he offered. I looked out the window at the gray, dreary day and told him that would be good.

By the third week of school, I could think up several things I'd rather do than continue my sixth grade education, but I "boldly persevered," as Violet Hayes's knight with the silver sword would say. What else was there for me to do? Homeschooling was not exactly an option.

During those first couple of weeks, my ex-friends seemed to go out of their way not to cross my path. Whenever I came near them, they'd just turn their heads and start talking to one another. Or they'd suddenly pretend to be very interested in something else, like their nail polish or boys walking down the hall. I wondered what was going through their minds. Had they made a pact to pretend that I didn't exist? Were they talking about me behind my back?

Meanwhile, I think that most of the other people at school started to get the impression that I was a loner, so I guess I'd accomplished my mission of being independent. But there didn't seem to be any prize for this as far as I could see. In fact, I felt like I was being punished.

I did manage to come up with some tricks for survival, however. One thing I discovered was that if I looked depressed enough in the mornings, my dad would take me to school even when it wasn't raining despite my mother's complaints that it was a waste of gasoline when I had a perfectly good pair of legs that needed more exercise anyway. Dad argued that he enjoyed spending a few extra minutes with me every morning. Actually, I was getting to spend more extra minutes — hours even — with my parents since the phone wasn't exactly ringing off the hook with invitations for me to go over to other kids' houses.

It was nice getting a ride to school, and it always lifted my spirits to have Nicholas, my Christmas tree–ornament gnome, with me. In the mornings when I was getting myself organized for school, I got into the habit of slipping him into the pocket of Beth's old Windbreaker (which Mom found and insisted I wear). Not only was he a reminder that I *did* have friends in the world, but he also helped me remember that no matter how bad things got, Christmas, my absolutely favorite holiday in the world, would always eventually come. I had already started to make a list of things I wanted, and NEW CLOTHES was at the top, right under KITTEN, which is something I always put there but knew I'd never get.

Another thing that made me feel more secure was not having to go braless any more. A few days after I called Mary Ann, I got a package from her with not one but three new bras, each a different color. They didn't look too old-ladyish, and two of them fit pretty well after I adjusted the straps. The other one would do in an emergency.

I know this sounds weird, but it made me feel more confident when I wore a bra to school. If there was some kind of freak accident or something and my shirt got ripped or my buttons popped open, it was good to know that I'd be "covered."

I didn't say anything to my mother about the bras, so there was an awkward moment when she found the white one in the clothes hamper and wanted to know where it came from. I just said, "Mary Ann sent it," and she gave me this puzzled, hurt look. I was afraid she was going to scold me, but she just folded it up and took it to the basement to wash.

With my new bras, my dyed-black clothes (which my mother continued to declare were ruined), and a couple of Cubs sweatshirts Dad bought me on the sly, my wardrobe was a lot less pathetic than it might have been.

At first, the worst times for me were after school on the days Dad couldn't pick me up. Knowing I'd have to walk home alone, I sort of dawdled at my locker until most of the kids were out of the building and well on their way home. Then, when the sidewalks were mostly empty, I strolled at my own pace, talking to Nicholas.

Sometimes, it kind of spooked me out not having any kids around to keep me company, but after a while I got used to it. I had plenty of time to think about whatever I wanted, and mostly I plotted how to convince Violet Hayes (who rode the bus) that we should be friends. The more I saw Violet, the more curious I was about her. She was different from anyone I'd ever met, and I was determined to get her to like me.

The main problem was that although Violet Hayes was an independent person like me, she was the type of independent person who didn't seem to need friends. Every morning she arrived to school early, sat down at her desk, and buried her nose in *The Knight with the Silver Sword*. Finally, in order to make her pay attention to me, I started asking questions about what was happening in her book. This was a mistake. Although Violet's descriptions of the knight's "valiant" efforts to save women and children from invaders might have been exciting to some people, it was so dull to me that I could hardly follow what she was saying. When I asked her how she got interested in knights, she brightened a little. Then she told me all about how at her old school in Vermont, she was a member of the Magic Castle Club (snore), which was for people who were into parading around in medieval costumes (double snore). They had fake duels with swords and played wooden instruments (triple snore).

Getting Violet to talk about anything more recent than the 1500s was like pulling teeth, but I did find out a little something about her family. Her mother owned the new health food store downtown, and her father was a professor at Mary Ann's college, which was kind of a coincidence, I thought.

When I told Violet that my sister attended University of Illinois, I saw a flicker of interest in her eyes.

"My dad probably knows her," she guessed. "He teaches a lot of medical students."

"Oh, yeah, probably." I wondered if this was God's way of punishing me for telling a lie in front of the class.

I'm not sure why, but after Violet learned about Mary Ann going to U of I, she warmed up to me a bit and became more willing to listen to what I had to say. She was particularly interested in the fact that I'd started taking violin lessons.

"Back in Vermont, I used to have a friend who played the violin," she told me.

Violet once had a friend? There was hope! I thought.

"Mandy and I used to play duets together," she explained. "I played the recorder, which is a medieval wooden flute. And sometimes we'd stay after school and practice in the stairwell."

An image of Violet playing duets with her friend flashed through my mind. Both of them had dark brown braids that hung down their waists. Both of them wore hiking boots and overalls with designs running up the sides.

"I wasn't too good at playing the recorder," Violet admitted. "But Mandy was *really* talented at violin. She could just look at a piece of music and know what it should sound like in her head."

"Cool."

Somehow, without really meaning to, I gave Violet the wrong impression about how advanced I was on the violin, and she started bugging me to bring it to school to show her.

"We could work on a duet, like Mandy and I used to," she suggested.

"Hm, maybe."

Although I thought that playing music with Violet might be a way for us to become better friends, the truth was that I wasn't exactly ready to perform in front of her. In fact, Mr. Keesly hadn't even let me touch the strings on my violin yet. I know I should have just told Violet the truth about not being able to play, but instead I eventually made up this dumb excuse that I was working on this very "complicated" song that I didn't want to share with anyone yet.

You'd think Violet would drop the matter, and that would be the end of that. But she was like a dog with a bone, going on and on about how wonderful it would be if we could work out a song together and perform at a medieval fair (like we even *had* a medieval fair in Hickory Grove). The more I tried to change the subject, the more stubborn she got until she finally wore me down. I agreed to bring my violin to school for her to see, but I told her that I would not under any circumstances play her a tune on school grounds.

The day I arrived at school with my black case, I literally sprinted from the car into the school, ignoring the stares from kids wondering why I was in such a hurry. What I didn't want to happen was to have some orchestra student notice what I was carrying and have them start asking nosy questions. I've got to admit that it bothered me that there were at least a dozen middle school students who could play actual melodies on their violins while I was still struggling with my bow hold.

Unfortunately, several people did notice my violin case. Beth was one of them, but thankfully, she didn't bother asking any questions. She just raised her eyebrows and turned her head away.

Another person who noticed was Brian Bailey, who did ask questions. When I stuffed my violin in my locker, there he was shifting from one foot to the other the way he does sometimes. I noticed he'd lost a little weight since I saw him that day at Dino's Pizzeria.

"I didn't know you played violin. Are you going to join the school orchestra?" he asked, flipping a few strands of hair out of his eyes.

"No," I answered quickly. "I just brought it to school to show someone."

"I bet you're really good. Too good for the orchestra here."

"No, really. I'm not."

The more I tried to convince Brian that I wasn't any good at playing violin, the more he — just like Violet — thought

I was being modest. The whole thing was getting really ridiculous. Finally, I managed to slip away from him and get into the classroom, but as soon as Violet saw me, she put down her knight book and joined me at my desk.

"Well, where is it?" she asked.

"Shh. It's in my locker. You can see it at lunchtime."

Disappointed, Violet went back to her seat.

❁   ❁   ❁

At 12:05, when most of Mrs. Lucas's students went running down the hall to the cafeteria, I pretended to look for something in my desk.

"If you're searching for your lunch, it's probably in your locker right next to your *violin*," Violet said, pushing up her glasses. I noticed she'd already gotten her lunch.

I continued shuffling papers for a couple of seconds until I was sure the coast was clear in the hall, then I dragged myself away from my desk and went to my locker with Violet trailing like a puppy close behind.

"Why don't you bring it to the cafeteria?" Violet asked while I fumbled with my lock.

"No, I can just show it to you here."

I swung open the door to my locker and stepped aside so Violet could have a look.

"Aren't you going to take it out of the case?" she asked.

"I guess." Gently, I pulled the violin case out of my locker, laid it on the floor, and unfastened the clasps.

"Is it okay if I touch it?" Violet asked.

"I guess so. Just be careful."

Eagerly, Violet ran her fingers up and down the neck of my violin, and I started feeling uneasy. I wasn't used to anyone besides me (and sometimes Mr. Keesly) touching it.

"It's a lot like Mandy's, except hers was darker," Violet said softly. Then she did something I never would have dared to do. She grabbed the A string between her thumb and first finger and pulled hard, making a loud twanging noise that echoed in the hallway.

"Watch it! You're going to break it!" I shouted.

Curious to see what was going on in the hall, Mr. J. poked his head out of his classroom and shot us a questioning look.

"Maybe we should move to the stairwell," Violet suggested.

"I don't think so," I said.

Just as I had imagined what Violet and Mandy would look like as they played duets in the stairwell, I now tried to conjure a picture of Violet and me there. Violet would look very musician-like in the outfit she was wearing today, a long cotton skirt and an embroidered peasant blouse. Next to her, I would look very un-musician-like in my shorts and Cubs sweatshirt, trying not to make too much noise or attract too much attention.

"I think there's a rule against hanging out in the stairwell at this school," I said. "We'd better get to the cafeteria or we might get in trouble."

"The schools in Illinois sure are different from the schools in Vermont," Violet replied sadly as I packed up my violin.

I didn't know if what Violet said was true, but I was beginning to think that there were a lot more things different about her and me than where we came from. Would we ever connect as friends? I was beginning to have my doubts.

NICHOLAS TAKES A SPILL

Thinking that I'd let Violet down, I was feeling kind of blue as we made our way to the school cafeteria. Neither of us felt like talking. Violet's mind was probably on Vermont and the wonderful times she'd had with Mandy. I was thinking about how dumb it was for me to pretend to know how to play the violin just to be Violet's friend.

At least with Beth, I didn't have to pretend anything. She might have teased me sometimes, and she definitely got mad at me and prodded me to do things I didn't think were fun, but she knew who I was. She knew all my flaws just like I knew hers. I didn't have to do anything to try to impress her.

It was foot-long hot-dog day in the cafeteria, and lines for lunch were really long. I regretted my decision to buy rather than bring my lunch that day. Since we were arriving so late, there was a good chance I wouldn't have time to go through the line, pay for my hot dog, and finish eating it before the dismissal bell rang.

While Violet settled down at our table near the cafeteria monitor with her sack lunch, I bleakly stood behind Kyle Jacobs. My stomach growled, and Kyle turned around.

"Was that you?" he asked.

"I'm hungry, okay?" I snapped.

I had a clear view of my ex-friends' table from where I was in line, and I noticed Beth whispering something to Jayne. Beth must have felt me staring at her because she suddenly looked my way. Our eyes met. Instead of turning away, she waved. I tensed, wondering why, all of a sudden, Beth was paying me some attention. Then she stood up and started walking toward me. Immediately, the other girls at the table formed a huddle, and Jayne was telling everybody something. What was this all about? Was Beth going to insult me about something, or was she going to invite me to eat at her table? I looked down at my feet, not knowing what I'd say if Beth wanted me to eat with her.

"Rissa?" Beth was holding something in her hand. "I think you dropped this before school this morning," she whispered quietly so Kyle wouldn't hear.

She opened her hand to show me what she had hidden in her palm.

I let out a little gasp. Nicholas! He must have fallen out of my coat pocket when I was lugging around my violin! I stood there dumbly, trying to absorb how close Nicholas had come to being lost until Kyle caught on to the fact something was going on and peered over Beth's shoulder.

"What's that? A doll?" He asked rather loudly. And all of a sudden Angel was there with Kerry and Jayne right behind her.

"Jayne told me what you found. Let's see." Angel plucked Nicholas out of Beth's hand, and turned to face me. "What are you doing with *this* at school, Rissa? Isn't this . . ." Angel let out a giggle. "Isn't this one of your GNOMES?"

"Oh, my God! It's your little Christmas tree–ornament gnome," Kerry piped. "I can't believe you still have him. Didn't you get him, like, when you were in first grade?"

Jayne shot Beth a worried look.

I was too stunned to say anything.

So was Beth.

"Hey, Bartholomew, I didn't know you were into gnomes," Kyle said.

He grinned, and I felt like slapping his face.

I held out my hand, hoping that by some miracle, Angel would give Nicholas back to me without saying anything else. But of course that was not to be the case.

Instead, Angel held up Nicholas by his pointed hat.

"I want a foot-long hot dog," she said squeakily, pretending that Nicholas was the one speaking. "And I looooove ketchup!" She took him over to the condiment table, and held him over the tub of ketchup, making it look like he was about to jump in.

"Oh, I've always wanted to swim in a pool of ketchup!" Kerry said, imitating Angel's squeaky voice.

"Give him back," I hissed. My heart was beating hard, not just because Angel was making a spectacle, but because I couldn't bear to see Nicholas humiliated or, worse yet, injured. He was inches away from being doused in ketchup.

Angel looked over at Beth, who was *not* smiling.

"Just kidding, Rissa. Here you go!" Angel threw Nicholas up in the air, but Kerry, who was a good two inches taller than me, reached up and caught him first.

"Keep away!" she screeched. "Here, Kyle." She tossed Nicholas in the direction of Kyle, who, let's face it, was not the most coordinated boy in sixth grade. He lunged awkwardly to make a catch. Nicholas ricocheted off his elbow and fell in the trash barrel next to the table.

Beth covered her mouth.

Angel doubled over with laughter.

Kerry yelled, "Two points, Kyle!"

Jayne looked startled.

By this time, we had attracted the attention of the spiky-haired lunchroom monitor.

"What's going on here?" she boomed, as the girls scattered in different directions.

"Kerry McGrew threw Rissa Bartholomew's doll in the trash can," Kyle reported.

"Her doll?" The monitor shot me a puzzled look.

"It's a gnome," I said quietly.

The lunch monitor still looked confused.

"Well, do you need help finding it?" She glanced around the cafeteria, looking for the guilty culprits who'd played keep-away with Nicholas, but the girls, once again abandoning me at a crucial moment, were gone.

"Never mind, I don't need any help," I told the lunch monitor. I marched over to the can and began digging through dirty wrappers and half-eaten pieces of fruit. At this point I was so upset with my ex-friends and so concerned that Nicholas might have gotten broken that I stopped caring what other people thought of me, burying my arms in garbage.

The bell had already rung before I finally found Nicholas, resting between an apple core and a half-eaten hot dog. Thank goodness, he was all in one piece. I picked him up, rubbed him off with a wadded-up napkin, gave him a *huge* apology, and jammed him into the pocket of my shorts.

By this time, almost everyone had filed out of the cafeteria. But Violet was still lingering by our table.

"Did he get hurt?" she asked.

"I don't think so, but thanks for asking," I said, thinking that if she was *really* my friend, she would have helped with the rescue.

CHAPTER 13

MENDING

On my way home from school, I walked faster than usual, not thinking about anything besides the day's events. It was like anger was propelling me on my way. How dare Angel grab Nicholas! How dare Beth disappear on me! How dare Violet pluck my violin string without even asking permission.

I'd had a miserable afternoon. For one thing, I was starving since I never did get my foot-long hot dog for lunch. For another thing, Nicholas's pointed hat kept poking me all through science, math, and art. But my pain was probably nothing compared to his. I figured that he must be feeling *really* uncomfortable, squeezed inside the pocket of my shorts, filmed with grease (and whatever else he might have picked up from the garbage can).

After school, when the corridors were finally empty, it

was a tremendous relief to get Nicholas out and rinse him off in the girls' bathroom (once I was sure it was empty). But when I returned him to my coat pocket, he fell straight down to the floor, and it was then that I discovered the hole. Instead of putting him in my other pocket, I zipped him inside my violin case just to be on the safe side.

❀   ❀   ❀

As soon as I got home, I made myself a peanut butter sandwich, which I wolfed down in about four bites. As I ate, my mother poured me a glass of milk.

"Maybe you're about to have a growth spurt," she commented.

"Probably." I didn't tell her I hadn't eaten lunch.

"Well, slow down or you'll get the hiccups." She handed me the milk, and started spreading peanut butter on another slice of bread.

"I have a hole in my coat pocket that needs to be sewn up," I told her.

"You do? Have you been jamming your hands in your pockets again?"

"No." I didn't tell her that the hole was probably the work of Nicholas's pointy hat.

"I can probably fix it this weekend. I have some other mending I have to do."

"Can't you do it sooner?" I pleaded.

"You're perfectly capable of using a needle and thread. The sewing basket's in my closet."

I scurried upstairs, before Mom could tell me how she did *all* her own mending when she was my age.

Despite the fact I wasn't the best seamstress in the world, sewing had a soothing effect on me. As I sat on my bed, triple stitching my pocket to make it extra strong, I was reminded of the times Beth and I made doll clothes and gnome clothes from scraps of cloth my mom gave to us. Once we made a dress for Beth's cat, Motormouth, but we couldn't get it on her because she hissed and fought so much. *Those were the good old days,* I thought. When life was simple and fun (well, maybe not for the cat), and I didn't have to worry about being humiliated in the school cafeteria or doing crazy stuff like bringing a violin to school to try to get someone to like me.

By the time I was done tying my final knot, I felt mellower, and my mind had cleared enough for me to realize the day could have been a lot worse.

If Beth hadn't found Nicholas, he might have stayed lost forever. I had to admit that it was nice of her to pick him up and keep him safe, and I hadn't even thanked her. I should have. I would have if Angel hadn't grabbed him.

Then I remembered how Beth had frowned at Angel

when she was threatening to douse Nicholas in ketchup. What did that frown mean? Was Beth trying to stand up for me to Angel in a way she hadn't at my birthday party? Was she turning more courageous?

It was too bad friendships couldn't be mended as easily as pockets, I thought.

Feeling a little sleepy and sad, I put away the thread and needle and caught sight of my mother's battered old sketchbook in the bottom of the sewing basket. I took it out and lay down on the bed to revisit my childhood (or at least the fashion part of it). As I leafed through pages of little-girl dresses, play sets, and bathing suits, I could just hear Mom saying, "Come here, Rissa. Do you think this is something you'd like to wear?"

I came across the picture of the Cinderella dress that Mom had made for me in kindergarten. It turned out so good that Beth had thrown a tantrum, saying she wanted one just like it.

"What do you think, Nelson?" I asked, holding up the book for him to see.

He thought I had a pretty talented mom.

I felt a lump form in my throat as I remembered the times I'd fought with my mother back in grade school, telling her how nobody else in my class "*would be caught dead*" wearing something *their* mother made. Was I wrong to tell her that? Was I just being mean and stubborn? Mary

Ann had worn clothes Mom made until she was in her teens.

The thing was, deep down in my heart, I knew that I *still* didn't want to wear my mother's creations any more than I wanted to wear hand-me-downs. Both were styles picked out by somebody else, not me.

I let out a sigh, closed the book, and carefully tucked it back in the sewing basket. What was my style? I wondered. Did I even have one?

CHAPTER 14

THE SOCIAL STUDIES PROJECT

As the next couple of weeks dragged by, I felt like I was standing still while all the other kids at school were whirling in different directions. After figuring out that I wasn't a "talented" violinist like Mandy and discovering I carried around a gnome, Violet seemed to lose interest in me. She became even more absorbed in her book.

Other people — even some of whom I'd thought were outcasts on the first day of school — started joining clubs and teams. Brian Bailey started hanging around with the orchestra kids. Kyle Jacobs found his niche in science club.

I watched from a distance as other kids found places where they belonged. It didn't take long for the popular girls from all the four grade schools to corral themselves together into one very loud and flashy crowd. Some of the other students, who were not in the popular crowd, came together because they had common interests. There were the kids who were really into drama, but I'd had enough drama at home with Mary Ann to want to join that group. I wasn't athletic enough to be one of the jock girls, and I *knew* I didn't fit in with the Skimpy-top girls who wore tons of makeup and didn't care if their bra straps hung out.

I don't know. Maybe things would have been different for me if there was a group of gnome collectors at my school, but gnome collecting wasn't what you'd call a popular hobby at HGMS, although Kyle Jacobs *had* started calling me "Gnomey" and had given me an article on gnome mythology, which he'd found on the Internet.

There was only one thing I could think of that connected me to all my classmates, and that was our common problem of having too much homework. It was becoming clear that just like everybody said, more was expected of you in middle school than in grade school, especially if you had Mrs. Lucas for language arts and social studies. "Never settle for adequate. Aim for excellence!" was Mrs. Lucas's motto. (At least that was a little more original than "Don't follow the herd.")

A lot of kids thought Mrs. Lucas was too strict, but even though she'd made that comment about Mary Ann being a chatterbox, I kind of liked her. Mrs. Lucas was the type of teacher who didn't choose favorites, and she didn't zero in on just one kid to pick on the way some teachers (namely Mr. J.) did. Mrs. Lucas picked on everyone. It didn't matter how smart you were, how athletic you were, or how popular you were (or weren't). She treated everyone the same, and she *definitely* had no pets. Nearly every kid in the class had been accused of having a pea brain at least once. Actually, it was almost an honor to be called a pea brain. At least it meant you were being noticed.

There were some other good things about Mrs. Lucas, besides her treating everyone the same way. She was a good storyteller and she could explain things in an interesting way. Social studies, which I'd always hated before, was more bearable now because Mrs. Lucas made far-off places seem close by and familiar. Sometimes she'd show us souvenirs she'd gotten during her travels and sometimes she did these PowerPoint presentations, flashing up pictures of places she'd visited. In one slide, Mrs. Lucas was waving to us from the front of the Leaning Tower of Pisa. She was wearing these bright plaid shorts and a really dorky sun hat. It took a lot of guts to show a picture like that, and it made me respect her all the more.

When our class had finished studying maps of Europe and had a test on correctly identifying all the countries by their shape and location on the map, Mrs. Lucas announced that we'd be doing oral reports on the European countries that we'd studied. I groaned right along with everyone else, but really I was kind of excited. I love doing oral reports. I know how to make my voice carry and I'm usually pretty confident when talking in front of the class.

I hoped I'd get to do my report on Germany. That's where my grandparents are from. With any luck, I could get all my information from them without ever having to crack open an encyclopedia or go to the Internet. And I could use Pip, my wooden gnome from Germany, as a visual aid.

Mrs. Lucas passed out lists of Do's and Don'ts for the reports so there would be "no excuses for not knowing what was expected." Skimming the list, I was happy to see that visual aids were encouraged, but I was disappointed to see that we were expected to use at least two outside sources for the written part of the report. I doubted that Mrs. Lucas would accept Grandpa and Grandma Bartholomew as my two sources.

While everyone was looking over their lists, I glanced over at Beth, knowing what she was thinking about the Do's and Don'ts. She would look forward to writing the neatly printed notes on index cards that were required. Mrs. Lucas's reminders — DON'T SPEAK TOO SOFTLY and DON'T JUST *READ* YOUR NOTES — were probably making her nervous. Unlike me, she hates to speak in front of the class.

When I was staring at Beth, there was a sudden buzz of excitement in the classroom. Apparently, Mrs. Lucas had said we could do the project with partners and some people were already jumping out of their seats to claim who they wanted to work with. Jayne Littleton rushed over to Beth's desk. I tried to get Violet's attention, but she was busy talking to the girl who sat next to her. If Violet was going to be partners with her neighbor, who would I be with? I swallowed hard, wondering what to do next. Suddenly, the room felt too warm. Out of the corner of my eye, I saw Brian Bailey get out of his seat and move in my direction. Leave it to good old Brian. He'd bail me out and ask to be my partner. But he did not stop at my desk. He headed on to Kyle's desk, and the two of them started talking about working together. Now the room felt downright hot, and I remembered that Julie Campbell was absent. Would I end up being Julie's partner because nobody else wanted me? Julie had several friends in our class. Would she be mad that she got stuck with me? I could feel tears starting to come and looked down at the instruction sheet to distract myself.

DO BE A COOPERATIVE PARTNER, I read. TEAMWORK WILL COUNT FOR 25% OF YOUR GRADE.

Then someone poked me on the shoulder.

"Do you want to do the report together?"

It was Violet. I felt like standing up and hugging her. I didn't care if someone else might have rejected her for a partner. I didn't care if I was her second choice. I didn't care if I sounded too desperate when I said, "Sure, we can work together," as I grabbed her sleeve to show everyone that she was *my* partner and no one could have her. "What country do you want to do?" I said in a rush of relief. "I was thinking Germany would be fun."

"We don't get to choose," Violet answered sullenly, pointing at the final Don't on Mrs. Lucas's list, which read: DON'T COMPLAIN ABOUT THE COUNTRY THAT YOUR TEACHER ASSIGNS TO YOU.

Being characteristically "fair," Mrs. Lucas decided that we'd draw names of countries from the gigantic coffee mug that never leaves her desk. Now that my wave of panic had left, I kind of enjoyed the suspense of wondering what country Violet and I would pick. Tension mounted as partners marched up to the teacher's desk to choose their fate.

Kyle and Brian got Switzerland. Next it was our turn. I concentrated hard on Germany and put my hand in the mug.

"What did you get?" Violet asked as I opened the slip of paper.

"Turkey," I said with surprise.

I guess things could have been worse. We could have gotten Bulgaria, or I could have been walking down the aisle to the coffee mug alone. But on the other hand, things could have been better, too. It would have been nice if someone besides Beth and Jayne had ended up with Germany.

CHAPTER 15

VIOLET'S HOUSE

I've always had this suspicion that there's some kind of secret network among mothers. Maybe they exchange information on the computer or something. Maybe there's a weekly newsletter giving all the dirt about what's going on in the neighborhood or maybe they take turns spying on each other. I don't know for sure how they do it, but the moms in my town — especially Mrs. White, who *runs* the network, I suspect — are always in the know. For example, somehow all the mothers knew that Kyle Jacobs has a genius IQ and was also a bed wetter until age eight. They were also aware that Kerry was a level-nine gymnast (something I didn't even know until my mother told me), and I was pretty sure that it had become common knowledge among all mothers that Beth wanted to be called Bethany.

Anyway, to get to my point, I figured Mom had probably heard of Violet Hayes, but I didn't expect her to be a walking encyclopedia of the Hayes family history. Somehow, through the mysterious network, Mom had found out that they came from Vermont. She knew all about Dr. Hayes teaching at University of Illinois and how his wife opened a health food store downtown. Mom had actually gone there with Mrs. White to buy some free-range eggs, which tasted a lot like regular eggs but were a lot more yellow.

Anyway, since Mom already met Violet's mother and was aware of her father's occupation, I figured that Mom wouldn't have any questions to ask about Violet when I told her that we were social studies partners. But I was wrong.

"So, how's Violet liking Illinois?" she wanted to know. I'd been home for an hour or so and was eating a bag of fruit snacks at the kitchen table while Mom cleaned out the refrigerator.

"I think she misses Vermont," I said.

"It must be quite an adjustment for her, living out here." Mom paused to check the expiration date on a carton of yogurt.

"I guess so." I half expected my mother to ask if Violet had done anything about starting a Magic Castle Club or was still missing her old friend, Mandy, but instead she said, "I'm sure you two will work very well together, but . . ."

"But what?"

"What about Bethany? I thought you two usually teamed up for projects."

This was true, of course. My mind raced back to all of the maps and models Beth and I had done together. Last year we built a circuit board for the science fair. In second grade we made a poster of the food pyramid. I did the hard part, outlining everything, and I let Beth do the fun part of coloring in.

"We're not working together this time," I said.

"Oh, I see." Mom put the yogurt back on the shelf, closed the refrigerator door, then turned around to face me. "Don't you think this feud you're having with Beth has gone on long enough?"

"We're not having a *feud*," I said. To me, feuds meant shouting (and perhaps a shotgun duel), not long stretches of silence.

"When Mrs. White and I were friends back in high school, we had some feuds," she confided. "But we always made up after a few days."

I tried to imagine my mother and Mrs. White as teenagers. I could see them walking down the hall at school, Mrs. White in the lead, my mother following meekly behind. If there were any shouting matches, I was pretty sure Beth's mom had the advantage.

"What did you fight about?" I asked.

"Oh, silly things. You know how testy Beth's mother can get."

"Did you fight over boys?"

"I don't remember. It was a long time ago."

"But you always ended up being the one to apologize, right?" I could see it all so clearly. Mrs. White acting huffy. My mom trying to make amends.

"Well, not *always*," Mom insisted, but her face turned pink, so I guessed that she'd done way more than her share of smoothing things over after a fight.

On our way to Violet's house, Mom drove really slowly. I kept getting the feeling she wanted to say something more about the "feud" between Beth and me, and maybe give me some advice about how I should beg and plead to be Beth's best friend again, but she kept quiet. The silence between us wasn't an angry one. It was more of a thoughtful, uneasy one. Mom was so distracted that she missed Violet's house altogether and had to drive back around the block to reach the house where the Hayeses lived. For a minute, we just sat in the car staring.

"Well, this is an interesting house," Mom finally said.

"Incredibly cool" is what I'd have called it. The house, painted lavender, was really old and huge. It had a big wrap-around porch, but the best part about it was that it had this little round tower on one side. That had to be Violet's room, I figured. She seemed like the type of girl who might sleep in a tower.

"I'll pick you up at four," Mom reminded me. "Call if you want to come home earlier."

✿ ✿ ✿

It was kind of creepy standing by myself on the Hayeses' front porch. As I peered through the wavy glass window, it came as a relief to see Violet and not some Lurch-type butler coming to answer the door.

Once I was inside the high-ceilinged entry hall, I instantly regretted that we would have to spend the morning gathering facts about Turkey. I would rather have spent time exploring the Hayeses' big house, especially Violet's tower room, which I imagined would have a canopy bed.

"I like your house," I told Violet.

"I liked the one we had in Vermont better," she replied. "But I guess this one's okay."

"It kind of reminds me of a haunted house. How old is it?"

"About a century," she said, taking my Windbreaker and hanging it on a coatrack near the door. "I guess our house is all right," she said, squinting at a crack in the wall. "But there's a million things to be fixed and there are way too many rooms."

How could someone complain about having too *many* rooms? I wondered. I was always wishing that we had an extra bathroom upstairs or a rec room with a large-screen TV like the Whites had. I'd go nuts with excitement if I got to live in a house like this one, but I was coming to understand that Violet Hayes got excited about very few things that didn't have to do with medieval times. I guess the house would have to be about 500 years old and have a drawbridge and moat to make her happy.

"Can I see your room?" I asked eagerly.

Violet took me upstairs, not to the tower room as I thought she would, but to a very ordinary square room that looked like anybody else's, except it was unusually neat and there were more bookcases than you'd expect in a bedroom. A plain, dark green comforter covered the bed. Matching curtains hung from the windows. Violet didn't have any posters on the wall, but there were two large framed pictures. One was of a mountain; the other was a fairy-tale scene that looked like Rapunzel letting down her hair or something. I noticed that Rapunzel had gotten some highlights.

The most interesting thing in the room was the ring of photographs stuck into the frame of Violet's mirror. I stepped closer, hoping to see a side of her in the pictures that was kept private from the rest of the world. Violet was one of those types of people who, as my mother would say, was a hard nut to crack. Her quietness made me believe she had secrets.

Most of the photographs were of strangers and didn't have any meaning to me. There was one showing a man who looked about my father's age and a woman who looked a lot younger.

"Your parents?" I guessed.

Violet nodded.

"Are they home?" I thought it was a little odd that I hadn't met Mr. or Mrs. Hayes yet.

"Dad is. Mom's working at the store."

"Oh."

I glanced over the rest of the photographs and finally found one with Violet in it. She was standing next to a girl with a violin. Both girls were grinning, which I found a little jolting. I wasn't used to seeing Violet smile. As far as I'd known, she had only two facial expressions. There was the Violet Hayes with her lips in a straight line with a smooth forehead, which was the Violet I saw most of the time. Then there was the Violet with her lips in a straight line with a wrinkled forehead when she was concentrating hard on something, like a math problem.

It was too bad she lost her smile when she moved to Illinois, I thought. Then I thought about how I hadn't been doing much smiling lately, either.

"Is that girl in the picture the one who played duets with you on the violin?" I asked.

"Yeah, that's Mandy." Violet didn't offer any more information, and I got the impression that she didn't want me to ask any more questions.

I took a closer look at the photograph, trying to detect what it was about Mandy that made her such a good friend.

"We'd better go downstairs," Violet said abruptly. "My dad's working up here in his study, and I told him we wouldn't be noisy."

Noisy? By my standards, Violet and I were talking very quietly, but it looked like I wasn't going to get to see the tower room, so I followed her back downstairs to a room that was lined with more bookshelves. The Hayeses sure liked to read, I thought.

"We should get going on the report," Violet reminded me. She pulled out a folded piece of paper from her pocket, which turned out to be Mrs. Lucas's list of Do's and Don'ts.

"What do you want to work on first?" I asked her.

"I guess we should find our two sources first. My dad's using the computer, so we can't go online, but we could look up information in books."

"Or we could work on something else," I suggested, thinking that anything would be more fun than poring over some dull books about Turkey. I looked over Violet's shoulder at the assignment sheet she was holding.

"We could prepare a national food for extra credit," I suggested. So far, Violet hadn't offered any kind of snack and I was starting to get hungry.

"We'd get five extra points for that," Violet noticed, reading the bottom of the sheet. "And my mother has lots of cookbooks. Let's go look for recipes."

This was the most enthused I'd seen Violet since my arrival at her house. I followed her into the kitchen, which was like the kind you see in magazines and movies with pots and pans hanging from the ceiling and about a hundred different kinds of knives sticking out from blocks of wood.

On one side of the room was yet another bookcase. This one was filled with about every kind of cookbook you could imagine. Violet pulled out two and handed me one of them. It was called *Mediterranean Delights* and had a lot of lamb recipes.

"Do you like lamb?" I asked Violet. "I don't."

"We don't eat much red meat." Now Violet was wearing her concentrating-very-hard expression with her forehead all wrinkled up. I wondered if she was finding any good recipes in her book and hoped she was looking in the dessert section.

"Find anything for Turkish taffy or Turkish delight?" I asked. Those were the only Turkish foods I knew.

"I think my mom has all the ingredients for stuffed eggplant," Violet mumbled, ignoring me.

"What's it stuffed with?" I asked. Stuffed eggplant wouldn't have been my first choice of food to bring to school, but I was trying to be a good sport.

"The stuffing is mostly rice."

That sounded safe enough. Violet, who seemed very at home in the kitchen, started pulling out ingredients and measuring utensils.

"Are you sure it's okay with your mom that we do this?" I asked. I was thinking how my mother would never let me cook something major like stuffed eggplant without supervision. If Violet was at my house, Mom would be chasing after us with a wet sponge, cleaning up spills and giving us pointers.

"I cook by myself all the time," Violet said. She pulled out two eggplants from the refrigerator and handed them to me. "We can make a couple of batches and freeze them until the day of our report. It's supposed to be good hot or at room temperature."

She seemed to know an awful lot about food, I thought. I guess a person would if their mother owned a health food store.

As instructed by Violet, I microwaved the eggplant and scooped out the insides. She focused on the more complicated job of making rice stuffing. I got done first, so I watched Violet as she stood over the stove stirring the rice and got to thinking about how she was different from any kid I'd ever met. In some ways Violet seemed much older than me. She could do as she pleased without parents hovering over her, checking to make sure she didn't screw up. She knew how to cook without making a big mess. She probably would have known how to clean out the washing machine after I'd dyed my clothes. It was too bad she wasn't with me at my house that day.

But in other ways, Violet seemed younger than her age. She didn't know anything about the latest fashions or hairstyles. She didn't wear lip gloss like most of the girls at school, and I'd never seen her wear nail polish.

One thing was for sure. She was the most independent kid I'd ever met.

Violet looked up from the simmering rice. "Why are you staring at me?"

"I was just thinking about what it means to be an independent person."

If she thought that this was an odd subject to bring up, Violet didn't let on.

"There's this character in my book named Princess

Celia." She wrinkled her forehead. "Celia has a very independent spirit."

"What's she like?"

"She thinks for herself. And she likes *being* by herself in the woods."

"But it's no fun to *always* be by yourself," I pointed out.

Violet gave the rice a stir.

"Celia is kind of a rebel. She refuses to marry a handsome prince named Bertram. Everyone tells her that a curse will befall her if she doesn't, but she doesn't care. She doesn't listen to what anyone says."

"But what do you mean, she doesn't listen to what people say? What does she do, plug up her ears and hum to herself?"

"Of course not."

"And how can she just stop herself from caring?" I really wanted to know. If I had the skill of not listening or caring, it would make not being independent a whole lot easier.

"I don't know." Violet sounded a little offended.

"This Celia character sounds kind of phony to me," I said. "I bet she just pretends not to listen or care. I bet she stays up nights sweating over that curse that's bound to drop down any second."

"She does not," Violet said defensively. "Celia is a brave heroine."

"But in real life, there are some people you have to listen to, like your parents, for instance. Like when they tell you what to do." My mind was starting to stray far from Celia in the woods. I was thinking of myself in the bathroom at my birthday party. If my mother had said I absolutely *had* to go back and join the party, I would have gone back in a flash.

"My parents aren't into telling me what to do. They trust me to make my own decisions. They let me be an independent spirit like Celia. Besides, they're too busy with their jobs to be looking over my shoulder every second." Violet turned off the stove and put a lid on the rice pan.

"What about your friends back in Vermont? Didn't you listen to stuff *they* said? Didn't you listen to Mandy?"

Suddenly, Violet's eyes were clouded with sadness, and I knew I'd hit a nerve.

"We sort of drifted apart."

I waited for her to tell me more. But she remained silent, leaving me to guess why she and Mandy parted ways. Maybe they had a falling-out like Beth and me. I wondered if Violet had felt betrayed.

"What was Mandy like? I mean, before you drifted apart," I asked, wondering if she'd turned into a mall-oholic like Beth.

"She was into medieval stuff like me. And she was really

smart. Not just at history and playing music, but at math and science and a whole lot of other stuff, too."

"Then what happened?"

"Nothing. We just went different ways." Violet started putting away spices and I knew the subject was closed for now. I felt bad for Violet, letting a friend as cool as Mandy slip away, and I felt a wave of uncertainty about myself. I had this sinking feeling that I would never measure up to Mandy. Why would Violet want a friend like me, who was boring, untalented, and pathetic enough to pretend to know how to play the violin? To Violet, I was just a social studies partner. *She'd probably be happier doing this project alone in the woods,* I thought.

I guess it was kind of a weird coincidence that after I'd convinced myself that Violet didn't care one way or the other about me, she ended up saving my life. Okay, that's an exaggeration. This is what really happened.

While we were waiting for the stuffed eggplant to bake, we decided to eat the leftover stuffing. Not my idea of the most appetizing snack in the world, but it was there and I was hungry. I actually ended up eating twice as much as Violet did, and that was a GIGANTIC mistake. If I'd just tried a little taste, maybe things would have turned out differently.

It only took a few seconds before I started to feel funny and I suddenly found it hard to breathe. Then my skin started to itch. When I looked down at my arm, I saw a cluster of red bumps.

"There wasn't any tomato in the rice, was there?" I asked Violet, hoping that what was happening wasn't what I thought was happening.

"Just a little sun-dried tomato. OH, MY GOD!" It was then I realized Violet had a third facial expression. One of complete shock. Her mouth dropped open. Her eyes got wide. "What happened to your face?" she shouted. "Your cheeks are all spotty!"

"Tomatoes. I can't eat them," I managed to sputter despite the fact I was beginning to feel like a balloon inflating and my throat was starting to feel really tight.

"DAD!" Violet screamed.

She ran out of the room, leaving me to suffer all by myself. I didn't want to be alone. I wanted someone to be there with me. I wanted my mother. I wanted my gnomes. I wished I had the strength to go fetch Nicholas from my coat pocket.

The next thing I knew, Violet was back in the kitchen with a man who looked like he just woke up from a nap. A piece of his bushy hair was standing straight up, and his shirt was only half tucked in. He took hold of my chin and asked me to open my mouth, and while my mouth was open, he asked if I was having trouble catching my breath.

"Yesh," I managed to utter. I think he got the message.

"You two get into the car while I find my keys. We're going to the hospital," he said.

"Cush you call my mudder and tell her what haffened?" I wheezed to Violet, who stood in the corner of the room, her eyes still wide with fear.

Having temporarily lost her ability to speak, Violet nodded her head, picked up the phone, dropped it, retrieved it, and managed to punch the right numbers as I told them to her.

"Hello, Mrs. Bartholomew? Meet us at the hospital!" She squeaked, then tossed the phone on the table and ushered me to the car. Violet wasn't exactly clear explaining things to my mom, but I was pretty sure my mother would be waiting for us at the hospital when we arrived.

CHaPTeR 16

VISITORS

Everything that happened at the hospital is kind of fuzzy in my mind. I remember feeling relieved that I didn't have to take off my clothes. (I was wearing the bra from Mary Ann that didn't fit so well.) I remember lying on this little bed in the emergency room and the doctor — no, maybe it was a nurse — gave me a shot. The whole time, voices were running through my head.

My mother saying, "Everything's going to be all right."

Violet saying, "She thinks for herself. And she likes being by herself in the woods."

Someone offered me a Popsicle, I think.

Once I was home in my own bed, Mom and Dad fluttered around, getting me stuff. Dad unhooked the portable TV in the kitchen and set it up in my room. The reception was pretty lousy since there was no cable line upstairs, but it was a nice thought. Mom kept asking me if I wanted her to read me a chapter from my library book, but all I really wanted to do was rest in bed.

Around the time I was starting to feel bored, Violet phoned to see how I was.

"Do you still have hives?" she asked nervously. I guess I'd be nervous, too, if someone had a near-death experience in my kitchen.

"The hives are still there, but I'm feeling better," I reassured her.

"I didn't know you had an allergy to tomatoes. Why didn't you say something when you saw me put them into the rice?"

"I didn't know those red things were tomatoes. I thought they were those things you find inside of olives."

"Pimientos?"

"I guess so." There was a long pause.

"Well, I'll see you at school tomorrow."

"Unless I stay home sick."

After talking to Violet, I felt more awake. Well, at least awake enough to feel sorry for myself. I swallowed to test my throat. It didn't hurt anymore. I took down my gnomes off their shelf and put them on my bed so they formed a line in front of Nelson. We had a long conversation about my ailments, and my gnomes were very sympathetic. Then I got out of bed to see if my spots had started to fade. They hadn't. I slathered on some of the lotion that the doctor had given me, then I got back into bed and did what anyone in my situation would have done. I imagined what would have happened if I'd died in the hospital, and who all would have come to my funeral.

Everyone in my family would be there, of course. Mary Ann would have sped home from Urbana even if it meant missing a class. Violet would be there, too, since she was the one who killed me. And there would be Beth, Jayne, Angel, and Kerry huddled together at the back of the church sobbing and carrying on because they felt SO guilty about being incredibly mean to me when I was alive. "If only we had a second chance," they'd be crying. "We'd make it all up to her! She was SO kind and considerate to everyone, especially Brian Bailey. . . . If only we'd realized what a great person she was sooner!!!" The image of all my ex-friends with red, blotchy faces cheered me up some, and when the doorbell rang, I was feeling good enough to go out and see who'd come by.

"Oh, Catherine, how thoughtful," I heard Mom say.

I should have known it would be Beth's mother at the door. She was always the first to appear in times of crisis. I'm not sure if it was because she was a very caring person or just because she was nosy, but in either case, she was probably bringing one of her cure-alls: homemade soup or that horrible Jell-O that she makes with little shreds of carrot.

Then I heard Beth's voice and Mom saying, "It's been ages since I've seen you, honey."

I ran back to my room and dove into bed.

Just as I expected, Beth — probably prodded by my mother — came trudging up the stairs and peered uncertainly into my room.

"Hi," I said weakly.

"Hi. My mother brought you some Jell-O. Uh, your mom said it was okay for me to come up here to visit you."

"That was nice of your mother to bring Jell-O," I said nobly.

"So, why'd you eat tomatoes when you know you're allergic to them?"

"It's not like I did it on purpose," I said, sitting up. Then I went on to give her the details about what happened at Violet's house. Actually, I could have been saying anything. Beth wasn't really listening. She was staring at my spots.

"Your face looks awful."

"I've got hives. It's not like they're catching or anything. The doctor gave me a shot to make them go away."

"I don't think it's working."

"He said it might take a while."

"How sick were you, anyway?" Beth asked suspiciously. "I mean, did you, like, almost *die* or something?" She picked up a stray sock off my floor and tossed it into my dirty-clothes hamper.

"I'm not sure how close I was to dying. I lost consciousness for a while." What I said was not a complete lie. I did fall asleep for a few minutes after the doctor gave me the shot.

"Remember how we found out about your allergy?" Beth asked. "I was over at your house after preschool. Your mom made us those bacon, lettuce, and tomato sandwiches for lunch, and you had that attack. Everyone thought you were choking and your mom gave you the Heimlich maneuver, but you still had trouble breathing." She paused to reenact my wheezing. "Your face got all red and puffy and spotty like it is now. Do you remember?"

"Yeah, sort of." For a moment our eyes met, but Beth shifted her gaze to Nelson the Gnome.

"Is this new?" Beth ran her hand over his head.

"I got him for my birthday."

"What'd you name him?" Beth was the only person who knew I named my gnomes.

"Nelson."

Beth lowered herself onto my bed, careful not to sit on any of my other gnomes, who still stood in a straight line.

"Hello, Nelson," she said. And for just a second, it felt

like old times. I waited for her to say she was sorry that I was sick and apologize for the way she'd acted at the birthday party and afterward, but she just sat there, stroking Nelson's hat.

"Did you ever find Nicholas in the trash can?" she finally said.

"Uh-huh. He's right here." I picked him off my pillow and held him up for Beth to see.

"I'm glad you got him back."

"Thanks for picking him up that day when he fell out of my pocket," I said.

Beth got off the bed and started wandering around my room. I wondered if she noticed that I'd taken down the picture of the two of us sticking our tongues out at the camera. It used to be on my dresser, but now it was at the bottom of my underwear drawer.

"Well, at least you got out of working on your report today." She sighed, glancing at the portable television my dad had brought upstairs. "Jayne and I spent the whole day at the library, trying to get ours ready. But we didn't get much work done. Mostly we just talked about the slumber party Angel's having the weekend after Halloween."

Then she gave me a look. Was she wondering if I was invited? Or was she rubbing it in that I wasn't invited? I wasn't sure which.

Seeing that I wasn't going to break down and beg to hear more about the party, Beth blurted out, "How come you're so different now, Rissa?"

Me, different?

"Seriously, Rissa. You used to be a lot of fun, but now you're so . . ." Beth paused, searching for the end of her sentence. "You're so *weird*. You're starting to be like that Violet Hayes girl."

Wham. That hit me hard. Of course she didn't know that I'd been thinking how Violet and I were nothing alike. Violet didn't seem to care whether or not she had any friends. I did care. Deeply. And that would never change.

"Violet's not so bad. At least she's loyal. She called to see how I was doing the *moment* I came home from the hospital," I told Beth, exaggerating only slightly. "But *you* wouldn't have known if I was dead or alive if your mother hadn't dragged you here to see me."

"That's not true!" Beth protested. "My mother would have told me if you were dead."

There was an awkward silence, during which time I pictured Mrs. White with her cup of coffee, whispering to Beth, "By the way, dear, I heard through the mothers' network that Rissa Bartholomew has passed on. We should get you a new outfit for the funeral."

"I didn't mean how that sounded," Beth said in a small voice.

"It's true that your mother is one of the first moms to find out news," I admitted.

"I don't know about that, but she's definitely the first one to spread it." Beth smiled.

Then the subject turned to both of our mothers and their embarrassing behaviors. We were on safe ground now. There was no more mention of Violet or Jayne or upcoming parties until Mrs. White interrupted us, telling Beth it was time to go.

"See you around, Rissa," Beth said, getting up off my bed.

When? I wondered.

After Beth left, I knew that there was no way I'd be able to sleep. I had too much to think about. I had to admit that it was nice seeing her and that confused me. I didn't know where we stood. Were we back to being friends or not?

I reached under my bed for my violin. Secretly, I enjoyed looking at it and cradling it when nobody was forcing me to stand up straight and tall and lift it high in the air like a torch. I took out my bow and started doing my exercises — up and down like an elevator, back and forth like windshield wipers. I was still holding on to it when my dad came into my room with my strawberry smoothie. It was the third time that day he'd gotten me one from Velvet Freeze.

"Well, look at that," he said, studying my hand. "Mr. Keesly would be very proud."

Startled, I looked down at my fingers, amazed that they had automatically curled into a perfect bow hold.

THE COVER-UP

My spots were still there the next day, but I didn't get any sympathy from my parents.

"The doctor said that there's no reason to stay home as long as you don't have a temperature," Mom reminded me while I was still in bed. She rested the back of her hand on my forehead, just to confirm I wasn't burning up with fever.

"Come on, get up." She pulled my comforter back and took hold of my arm. What was she planning to do? Drag me to middle school?

"But I still have *hives*. Everyone will think that I have a disease," I groaned.

"No one will think you have a disease," Mom assured me. "I'll go with you to school to explain things to your teacher." Immediately, I sat up in bed.

"No way. You're not coming with me. I'll go by myself."
The thought of Mom *click, click, click*ing down the hall of
the middle school was more than I could bear.

"Fine. You can go by yourself, but you *will* go to school."

Knowing I was beat, I let my body go limp.

"Just give me five more minutes, please."

Since plan A, "begging to stay home," hadn't worked, I
replayed plan B in my mind. It was something I'd invented
the night before when Dad was out getting my final
smoothie.

As soon as Mom went downstairs, I crept into Mary
Ann's bedroom (which was a lot tidier now that she was
gone). I started digging through her drawers, and it didn't
take me long to find what I needed: that jumbo-size tube of
concealer Mary Ann used to use whenever she had a pimple attack. The stuff was a little — okay, a lot — darker
than my skin, but not darker than my spots. When I put it
on my face, it looked a little odd — kind of thick and
cakey — but it looked better than having a face
full of spots.

I had to be careful not to smear my face when I got
dressed in my dyed-black jeans and matching turtleneck
sweater (which, if worse came to worst, I could pull up over
my chin). When I joined my parents in the kitchen, I was
careful to keep myself turned away from them as much
as possible.

"You look like a cat burglar," Dad said to my back. At least he didn't think I'd gone Goth. "Whatever happened to wearing dresses to school? When I was a boy, all the girls wore dresses. In fact, we all wore uniforms."

"Welcome to the new millennium, dear," my mother said drily. I could tell that the weekend crisis was taking a toll on everyone in the family because both my parents were a little on edge. I think Dad, who's almost always in a good mood in the morning, had made one too many trips to Velvet Freeze the night before.

I kept my head bowed as I ate my cereal, but my mother's eagle eyes didn't miss what I'd done to try to hide my spots.

"What on earth do you have on your face?" she asked. She reached over and touched my cheek, then rubbed a little blob of makeup between her fingers. Dad raised his eyebrows but didn't say anything.

"Careful! You're going to wreck it." Now I was the one getting edgy.

"Is this *makeup*?"

"I've got to wear something to cover the hives. I look like a freak!" I exclaimed. "And if I absolutely have to go to school, please, please, *please* don't come along to talk to my teacher."

Mom and Dad looked at each other, then back at me. I could tell that they were starting to wear down.

"Okay," Mom said, sighing. "Wear the makeup just this once. But I'm writing a note to Mrs. Lucas, and if you want a ride with your father, you've got to get going. *Now!*"

❀ ❀ ❀

First class period, English, seemed to last about a hundred hours. It didn't take me long to realize that I'd done something really stupid. When I lifted my head up from my work, everyone quickly looked away, like they didn't want me to realize they'd been gawking at my face. No one could concentrate on their work. Several students were accused of having pea brains. Exasperated, Mrs. Lucas finally gave up and instructed us to read silently for the rest of the period. Then she called me up to her desk, and everyone stopped reading to watch what would happen.

"Come closer," she commanded. I took a step closer. "Is that some kind of medication that you have on your face?" Mrs. Lucas squinted at me.

"It's makeup," I whispered.

"Well, it's distracting the other students. You need to go wash it off," she whispered back.

"My face is full of . . . spots," I stuttered.

"I know it is. I read your mother's note," she said. "But spots can't be as bad as — well, Rissa, to tell you the truth, it looks like your skin is peeling off."

Someone snickered. Embarrassed, I lowered my head like a scolded dog and left the classroom.

As I looked at myself in the bathroom mirror under the harsh fluorescent light, I could see why Mrs. Lucas called me up to her desk. My face really did look pretty awful. The makeup had caked and there were crevices around my eyes and around my chin. I looked like I don't know what. Maybe someone with leprosy. I grabbed a wad of paper towels and started scrubbing furiously, using water and soap from the dispenser to get the job done. My face felt raw when I was done, but as I feared, the hives were still there, redder than ever after all that rubbing.

While I was in the bathroom, someone — Violet or Beth or maybe even Mrs. Lucas — must have spread the word about what happened to me over the weekend because when I got back to class, the stares that met me seemed to be a little more respectful. People started asking me questions. Kyle Jacobs turned around in his seat and asked what type of injection I was given in the hospital. Jayne Littleton wanted to know if it was true that I stopped breathing and passed out. I actually didn't mind being in the spotlight now that everything was out in the open. I mean, it wasn't like my hives looked like big, oozing pimples. No one said "eeww" or "gross" or anything.

When the time came for our class to meet up with Mr. J.'s homeroom to go to PE, something very curious happened. Beth and Jayne walked me down the hall. We stopped to pick up Kerry and Angel, and all of a sudden it was like we were the old group again, just as if nothing had ever happened. Violet — no doubt wracked with guilt for poisoning me — walked behind us.

❀ ❀ ❀

I was very glad I wore my favorite bra that day because when we undressed for PE, Angel, Beth, Jayne, and Kerry crowded around me, oohing sympathetically when they saw the hives on my stomach.

"Didn't the Hayeses know about your allergy?" Angel asked, shooting Violet an accusing glare.

"No, it wasn't their fault. Really. It was an innocent mistake."

"A very *serious* mistake," said Kerry. "You could have died. I think your parents should sue them."

"I really don't think I would have died." I felt bad for Violet, who was avoiding looking our way as she tied her shoes.

"Why don't you run with us when we do our laps today?" Angel asked casually.

I could hardly believe my ears. This was the most she'd said to me since the day she kidnapped Nicholas. Was the gate surrounding my old herd starting to open? Would there soon be a space big enough for me to slip through if I wanted? My heart started beating faster. Maybe Angel would invite me to her slumber party, not that I'd go or anything.

Then my senses took hold.

"I usually run with Violet," I told the girls. I started to move in Violet's direction, but Beth held me back.

"We need to talk." She motioned the others to go on ahead. They swept past Violet, who was standing by the entrance to the gym, waiting for me.

"Look, Rissa," Beth said sternly. "You can't just go on being in a snit and pretending that you're so much better than everyone else." I wasn't sure what exactly she was getting at, but I didn't appreciate her thinking I was in a "snit."

"I'm *not* in a snit," I defended myself. "And I'm not 'pretending' anything."

"But you called us jerks."

"What? You mean at the birthday party?"

Beth nodded her head.

"You guys were acting pretty mean to me," I said. "And to Brian, too."

"We were not! *You* were acting mean to us. You ran away from the table and didn't come back. You didn't even say good-bye to anyone."

"I had my reasons."

Beth sighed. "Don't you get it, Rissa? This is your chance to make things all right again. I think Angel's gotten over being mad at you," she said. "Come run with us today. We can just forget all about the birthday party and what happened. It's history. Show everybody that you want to be friends again. Show them that you're not avoiding them anymore, okay?"

I was avoiding *them*? She had to be joking. But she looked pretty serious. Actually, she looked kind of desperate.

"Things aren't the same without you in the group. You know me better than everyone else," she explained. "I *need* you. You and I have hung out together ever since we were babies."

There was a minute — just a minute — I was tempted to do what Beth asked. I couldn't believe that she thought that I knew her better than the other girls did. All this time I'd been worrying that we didn't "get" each other at all. Maybe I'd been wrong. Maybe things could go back to normal. It all seemed so simple: Run with Beth and the others, and *poof*, I'd have friends again.

But I couldn't just go crawling back and leave Violet out, could I? Even if we never got to be as close as Beth and I once had been, I was not about to betray Violet the way

Mandy had betrayed her and the way Beth had betrayed me at the birthday party.

"I've got to run laps with Violet. She's expecting me," I said.

"Rissa," Beth said, lowering her voice. "You've got to stop hanging out with her. People are going to think . . ."

"What? That I'm weird?"

"That's not what I said."

"Yes, you did. Yesterday. At my house."

Beth blushed, and I knew she remembered how she'd accused me of turning weird like Violet. "Oh, just forget it," she said, then turned away and flounced out of the locker room, nearly bumping into Violet on her way. If you ask me, it looked like Beth was the one who was in a snit.

What I did, staying loyal to Violet and all, might seem like a really honorable thing to do, but my stomach certainly didn't feel very honorable. I had a pain in there that made me wonder if I'd done the right thing. Maybe I was making a whole lot more trouble for myself than was necessary for someone just trying to get through the sixth grade.

It was like I was being pulled in two directions. Half of me wanted to be Violet's friend. The other half of me wanted to go back to my old group, and I still didn't know where I *really* belonged.

"Want to get going?" I asked Violet, who was still hovering against the back wall. But when I approached her, she turned away.

"I'd rather run by myself today," she said, opening the door to the gym. And I was left by myself in the locker room, both halves of me unwanted.

CHAPTER 18

THE PROBLEM WITH PROCRASTINATION

As my hives started to fade, I went out of my way to be extra friendly to Violet to make up for what was said about her and her family while we were dressing for PE. But by Wednesday, I was growing tired of her not seeming to notice that I was being nice. We still ate lunch together, but things were pretty strained. Most of the time, Violet kept her nose buried in a book. Now she was on *The Knight with the Silver Sword, Book 2: The Quest Continues.*

"What happened to Princess Celia from the other book?" I asked, just to be polite. "Did she live happily ever after alone in the woods?"

"Actually, no. She got shot by an arrow," Violet said curtly.

"I'm sorry."

"It was a tragic accident, but at least the curse was lifted when she died."

I thought of Celia lying in the woods with an arrow stuck in her chest, and guessed this was what came from trying to be too independent.

"Don't forget that we still have to finish our oral report," I reminded Violet.

Neither of us had mentioned Turkey since the eggplant disaster, but time was running out. Mrs. Lucas had just given us a little lecture on how she expected everyone to be *absolutely* prepared by Friday even though most people would not do their presentation until the following week. Being fifth in line, I figured Violet and I were safe. Still, we were way behind most of the groups in planning our report. Some kids had already brought in posters for Mrs. Lucas's approval.

"You don't have to worry about the report. I've got most of the research done already," Violet informed me. "I did it Sunday night when you were sick."

"But this is supposed to be a *team* project," I argued. "You've got to let me do part of the work."

"Why don't you just come up with a visual aid? And you can bring the food samples. I wouldn't want to risk almost *killing* you again."

"Look, I never blamed you for making me sick," I said. "And anyway, I'm all better now. See?" I stuck out my arms. "Hardly any hives left at all."

"Some people seem to think it's my fault."

"But remember what you said about being independent like Celia? That means you shouldn't care what other people say, right?"

This made Violet pause and wrinkle her forehead. I had a suspicion that she was starting to realize what I'd already figured out: It's hard not to care what other people say, especially when they are saying some not-very-nice things about you.

"Okay," Violet relented, seeming to thaw a little. "We'll divide up the parts of the report equally." Now all business, she took out a pen and started scribbling on a napkin. "I've already drawn the map and made up note cards for these subjects." She flashed me the napkin, a record of her accomplishments thus far. "That leaves political leaders and national products for you to research, plus you need to come up with the visual aid and a national food." She wrote more notes on the napkin as she thought aloud. "Does that sound fair? I mean, I could do more if you need me to."

"It sounds fair, I guess." I was a little annoyed that Violet had jumped ahead and chosen all her topics without consulting me.

"I really need to get an A on this project," she added, handing me the napkin. "I mean, my parents expect me to get A's, you know?"

No, I didn't know. I thought her parents let her do whatever she wanted. What exactly was Violet trying to tell me? That she'd get in trouble if I blew my part of the report? That I might not be able to live up to her (and her parents') expectations?

"Don't worry. Oral presentations are one of the things I do best," I said.

I really meant to work on my report that night, but a lot of things came up. My violin lesson with Mr. Keesly went on longer than usual because he wanted to talk to my dad about a recital he was planning for November. The recital was something I was dreading. So far, I knew only one song, "Peanut Butter Cookie," on the violin. It consisted of me bowing each string to the rhythm of Pea-nut-But-ter-Cook-ie. Believe me, it was not a tune you would recognize, and it took a lot of fancy piano playing in the background to make it sound halfway decent. I could think of no worse embarrassment (except maybe wearing orange, cakey makeup to school) than performing "Peanut Butter Cookie" to a crowd of parents and other students, most of whom would probably be half my age.

Anyway, after we finally escaped from Mr. Keesly's house, Dad took me to Sweet Dreams, this really cool candy shop downtown, so I could get a bag of Turkish taffy to use for

my national food. I knew it was kind of a cop-out. I probably should have cooked some fancy Turkish dish or
something, but time was running out and I was sure
everyone in my class would enjoy candy a lot more than
something like stuffed eggplant.

Dad and I got home late and we ate dinner late, and after
that I had to read my assigned chapter in *The Adventures
of Tom Sawyer*, which is a really good book in case you
haven't read it. The only problem with it is it has a lot of
hard vocabulary words, and it's full of these incredibly long
sentences. (One of them has more than 100 words — I
know because I counted.)

Anyway, I ended up reading a little ahead because I was
at that really exciting part when Tom and Becky are lost in
a cave. I kind of lost track of time and page numbers. Before
I knew it, it was ten o'clock and I still hadn't done any
research for the report. I spent a few minutes hunting
around the house for note cards, but by the time I found
them in my mother's desk drawer, I was too tired to look
up any facts on the computer.

I had just changed into my pajamas when Mom came
into my room and eyed the stack of empty note cards on
my bed.

"When is your report due?" she asked.

"Friday," I mumbled.

Mom crossed her arms and raised an eyebrow.

"Rissa, you have to stop procrastinating." She flipped through the cards, checking to see if maybe I'd written down a useful bit of information about Turkey somewhere.

"Don't worry, Mom, I do my best work under pressure," I said, but she gave me that same doubtful look Violet had given me at lunch.

The next night after dinner, after I'd practiced "Peanut Butter Cookie" for about the millionth time, I was ready to get some real work done on my report. While my parents watched a movie downstairs, I got all set up in the computer room with fresh paper in the printer and my stack of note cards in my lap. Everything was pretty quiet, and I should have been able to concentrate on schoolwork, but other things besides Turkey kept running through my mind. I thought about how Beth had said I was going to turn out to be "weird" like Violet. What exactly did she mean? And why did it bother me so much? Was being weird *always* a bad thing? Was it worse than trying to look and act just like everyone else the way Beth always did?

I mentally rewound events back to the day we were assigned the project. What would have happened if I'd asked Beth to be my partner before she hooked up with Jayne? Then I started to wonder what would have happened if I ran laps with Beth and the others that day in PE. Was it worth it to keep trying to get Violet to be my friend? Clearly, she preferred the company of fictional knights and independent-minded princesses to me and thought I wasn't smart enough to pull my share of the weight for the oral report.

Instead of starting in on my research, I decided to use one of my note cards to make a list of "Good Things" and "Bad Things" about my life. I figured that would put things in perspective, but unfortunately, my columns turned out to be sort of uneven:

GOOD THINGS
1   My hives have finally disappeared.
2   I own 3 bras.
3   My gnomes love me.

BAD THINGS
1   Having Violet (maybe) think I'm too stupid to be her partner.
2   Not being invited to Angel's party (not that I'd want to go or anything).
3   Making a fool of myself by wearing Mary Ann's makeup to school
4   Picking Turkey for my report.
5   Having to be in a violin recital

I picked up my pencil and added something else to the "bad" column that was very hard for me to write. I wrote it in very tiny letters. This is what I wrote:

Okay, so now you know. Now the whole world knows. I *cared* that I wasn't popular and I wasn't afraid (well, not much) to admit it.

By this time, I was feeling very lonely. I wished I could IM someone, but Mom wouldn't let me have an account because she'd heard through the "mother network" that some eighth grader had been stalked by some really old guy she'd met on the Internet. I was allowed to e-mail friends, but unfortunately, I didn't have any friends left to e-mail except my sister, Mary Ann.

"*Dear Mary Ann,*" I typed. "*How is life in your new apartment?*"

"Rissa!" I nearly jumped out of my seat, not knowing that my mother was standing right behind me. Had she seen the good things/bad things list in my lap? I exited out of my e-mail account and slipped the list into my pocket.

"You scared me!"

"Are you done with your report?"

"Almost."

"Isn't it due tomorrow?"

"Probably not until Monday."

"You *might* have to do it tomorrow, though. Right?"

"Right."

"Get going on it. Now."

With Mom still peering over my shoulder, I Googled Turkey. In response, I got about a thousand recipes for Thanksgiving turkey. I was kind of tempted to see what "deep-fried" Thanksgiving turkey was all about, but Mom was still hovering, so I quickly revised my search.

"This would go a lot faster if you or Dad could look up a few facts for me in the encyclopedia," I hinted.

Mom hesitated. For a second I thought she might cave in and help me.

"It might go faster that way," she admitted, "but then it wouldn't be your project, would it?"

I could tell this was a hard thing for her to say. She must have noticed my disappointment because she edged closer and rested her hand on my shoulder.

"I'm proud of you," she said.

"For what?" Surely she must have noticed that my note cards (minus the one in my pocket) were still blank.

"For a lot of things. For trying new things this year, for reaching out to a new girl at your school, and for being so independent."

"Thanks, Mom," I said halfheartedly as she left the room.

✿　✿　✿

During the next hour, I actually did get some work done. After pulling up a few useless articles, I finally found a fairly readable page listing the current leaders of Turkey and explaining how the government was run. I filled up three note cards with information and looked for pictures to use for visual aids. I found a photograph of a really old Turk wearing a tasseled hat called a fez. It might be fun to make a fez out of cardboard and felt, I thought. I could put it on one of my gnomes and use him as a model of a Turkish citizen. But then someone would be bound to ask what gnomes had to do with Turkey, so I gave up on that idea.

In the end, I did something much less creative. I printed out a picture of whirling dervishes, famous Turkish dancers. By the time I'd glued the picture to poster board and had drawn a border of some of Turkey's most famous monuments (there aren't really very many in case you were wondering), I was ready for bed even though I wasn't *absolutely* prepared for the presentation. Before I left the computer room, I took my list out of my pocket and added something else to the "Good Things" side:

4   Mom's proud of me.

Given how my luck had been going, you can probably guess what happened the next day. To make a long story short, three people were absent from class. Violet and I had to do our presentation before we had a chance to review our note cards together or organize who would say what when.

Okay, okay, I know I should have been *absolutely* prepared, like Mrs. Lucas said, but Violet and I had already decided to practice our report over the weekend and we didn't think there would be any need to practice it before Friday. I mean, there is something to be said for saving your energy. There is such a thing as overworking something, which is what I was trying to convince my parents about the "Peanut Butter Cookie" song, which they made me play about a thousand times a day in preparation for my recital.

When our names were called, Violet looked over at me with that same horrified look that she gave me when she thought I was going to die in her kitchen. I guess I wasn't the only person who assumed there would be no way we would have to give our report until Monday.

"I'll do all my stuff first, then you go," Violet whispered frantically as we displayed my picture of whirling dervishes and the map of Turkey that she'd drawn.

Then Violet began speaking to the class in a clear, steady voice, and it became obvious that she'd rehearsed her speech. A lot. I relaxed a little and actually got caught up in an interesting story she told about cave dwellers in a place called Cappadocia. The class seemed really interested, too.

They were full of questions, and Violet knew all the answers.

Then my turn came. I took a deep breath, wishing I'd had time to memorize my notes or at least read over them. I'd scribbled stuff down so fast that my handwriting was kind of messy and there were a lot of words I couldn't read. Instead of having a clear, steady voice to match Violet's, my voice was soft and halting, stumbling over people's names. (You try to pronounce Prime Minister Recep Tayyip Erdogan's and President Ahmet Necdet Sezer's names right off the bat without stuttering!) I think my part of the report was about as long as the "Peanut Butter Cookie" song. I was very relieved when it was over and I could pass out the Turkish taffy, which didn't go over quite as well as I expected since they turned out to be as hard as rocks.

"Hey, on the wrapper it says these were made in Kansas City, Missouri. This taffy isn't very authentic," Kyle Jacobs commented.

I thought it was very rude of him.

"Girls, aren't you forgetting something?" Mrs. Lucas asked. Violet and I looked at each other. I thought we'd covered everything we were supposed to cover.

"National products," our teacher mouthed.

Shoot. National products were my responsibility. I'd forgotten all about them until now. Violet probably knew some. I tried to send her a telepathic message to answer the question. She didn't get it.

"Um, eggplant?" I said in a very small voice.

✿　✿　✿

We got a C-plus on the report, and I had something to add to the "Bad Things" column of my list:

7　Messing up my part of the report and ruining Violet's A average.

CHAPTER 19

VIOLET LETS LOOSE

There is nothing worse than hearing people buzz with excitement over something you can't or don't want to be part of. While I quietly went about my business at school, most of my classmates (even the Skimpy-top girls) exchanged news about Angel's slumber party, which was predicted to be the biggest bash of the year. The guest list seemed to grow bigger every day, and rumor had it that Angel had even invited some of the boys in our class to come over that night to watch movies.

The only person besides me who pretended to ignore Angel's big plans was Violet, who for reasons I don't think either of us understood, *still* ate lunch with me despite the fact she was hopping mad about the report. I guess, like me, she didn't have many choices for other places to eat. I mean, what was she supposed to do? Sit with Brian Bailey, the only person in sixth grade who remained friendly and kind to everyone, no matter what? And speaking of Brian Bailey, I think he was doing pretty well in the sixth grade. He had a regular group of kids to sit with at lunch, and they were always laughing about something or other.

Meanwhile, my table for two was very quiet. Not only did Violet hardly speak to me, she rarely even looked in my direction. I could almost see wisps of smoke rising above her head.

Violet had stopped reading her knight book. These days, she was reading a book called *European Studies* in a mad attempt to earn extra credit and raise her ruined social studies grade. If she was trying to rub it in that the C-plus she got was my fault, it worked. Now it was my turn to be wracked with guilt. After putting up with Violet's cold silence for a couple of days, I knew something had to be done.

"I think that we should talk to Mrs. Lucas about our oral report grade," I boldly suggested. It was Friday after school, and I was standing at Violet's locker, which was incredibly organized, unlike my locker, which I could barely shut. I had my jacket on, not because I was cold, but so I could reach in my pocket and hang on to Nicholas for support if need be. (I knew I probably should have stopped bringing him to school, but I assure you that I checked my pocket frequently to make sure the stitches were holding.)

"It's not like she would *change* our grade or anything." Violet finished putting her books in her backpack and zipped it up.

"Well, she might if I explained things."

"What would you say?"

"I'd say that you were absolutely prepared for your report and I was the one who screwed things up. Maybe she could lower my grade and raise your grade so it would still average out to a C-plus." I got a little choked up, thinking of my sacrifice, but Violet's expression didn't change.

"Maybe that would work," she said, wrinkling her forehead. Together, we went back to the classroom, where Mrs. Lucas sat at her desk grading papers.

"Did you girls need something?" Mrs. Lucas peered at us over her reading glasses.

"We wanted to talk to you about our social studies presentation," I said, surprised that my words were coming out much smoother than they had for my report. I gave Nicholas a little squeeze, took a breath, and confessed everything, telling Mrs. Lucas how I'd waited until the last minute to finish my part of the work and hadn't had time to practice the presentation, and how the only fair thing to do would be to give Violet and me separate grades. All the while, my teacher listened intently, folding her hands as if in prayer and looking me straight in the eye.

"Tell me, Rissa," she said when I was through talking. "How did you and Violet work as partners?"

This threw me off guard. I didn't know what to say. I mean, Violet and I didn't really work as partners except for the day I went over to her house, and that, as you know, did not end well.

"We worked together okay," I said uncertainly.

"What parts of the presentation did you plan together?"

Violet and I looked at each other.

"We sort of divvied up the topics and worked independently," I admitted.

"I see. Violet, do you have anything to add?" Mrs. Lucas looked over at Violet, who had remained silent during my whole speech.

"No," she mumbled.

"A big part of your grade was determined by your ability to work together as a team. I think both of you got grades that you deserved." Mrs. Lucas began straightening her desk, indicating that the conversation was over.

"Okay. Well, thanks." I wasn't sure what I was thanking her for.

"Yeah, thanks," Violet echoed.

"Don't worry, girls. Getting a C-plus isn't the end of the world."

I knew that, but did Violet?

"Here," Mrs. Lucas handed us sheets of paper. "This might cheer you up. I forgot to pass these out in class."

I glanced at the flyer, which had something to do with a Halloween contest, and stuffed it in my pocket, careful not to jostle Nicholas too much. Violet stood stiffly, holding her copy of the flyer with both hands.

"Come on, Violet. We should go."

"I missed my bus," she said solemnly. "I need to call my mother to pick me up."

"I'll go to the office with you to call."

We walked down the hall in silence. I knew I should probably say something comforting, but the thing was that I kind of agreed with what Mrs. Lucas had said. It was beginning to dawn on me that maybe the C-plus grade *was* both our faults.

While Violet talked on the phone to her mother, I studied her face, wondering what she was thinking and how she was feeling about what Mrs. Lucas had said. It was so hard to tell with Violet. She might be more furious than ever at me, or she might just be feeling embarrassed.

"Is your mom coming?" I asked as soon as she hung up.

"She can't leave work for another half hour."

"I'll wait with you," I said. We sat down together on the bench by the outer door, where we had a view of the parking lot. Violet gazed outside, her mouth a straight line.

"I'm sorry things didn't work out," I told her.

"I figured it wouldn't work." Violet sighed.

"And I'm sorry I messed up the report."

Violet bit her bottom lip and continued looking out the window. For a moment, she didn't say anything. Then, very slowly, she turned her head to look at me.

"It was my fault just as much as it was yours." Her voice trembled a little. She probably wasn't used to admitting she'd done something wrong, and I felt a rush of sympathy. She looked incredibly uncomfortable, sitting there so straight and stiff.

"It's just a grade," I said. "Remember what Mrs. Lucas said, how a C-plus wasn't the end of the world?"

"But grades are important to me." Violet blinked and looked down at her hands.

"There are things way more important than grades," I insisted, realizing that I was sounding just like my mother after Mary Ann got a D on her first college paper. I wracked my brain to remember what other words Mom had said to make my sister feel better.

"You'll do better next time," I told Violet.

Violet glanced up at me, confused, as though I was speaking a foreign language.

"Let's talk about something else," I suggested.

"What?"

Anything but medieval history, I thought.

"You could tell me about Vermont," I offered.

"What do you want to know?"

"What do you miss about it?"

"The mountains." Violet paused to think of other things. "The lakes, my grandparents, my old house." She probably could have gone on forever if I'd let her.

"There are some good things about Illinois," I said, trying to lighten the mood.

"Maybe, but I *really* hate this school."

So did I sometimes, but that was beside the point.

"Why do you hate it so much?"

"It's so different from my old school. We didn't have bells there, and we called our teachers by their first names. And we could go wherever we wanted — even outside the building — for lunch."

I tried to picture going to a school like that. I didn't think I could call Mrs. Lucas by her first name. I couldn't even imagine her having one.

"You just don't get it, Rissa," Violet said as though she were reading my mind.

Then she slid a finger under her glasses and wiped her eye. I couldn't believe it. Was that a *tear* I saw? Part fascinated, part horrified, I watched as Violet's normally pale complexion turned pink. Some people look sweet and helpless when they start to cry; Violet did not. Her mouth quivered. Her nose started to run.

"Come on." I grabbed her wrist and pulled her off the bench.

Once inside the girls' restroom, Violet took several minutes to regain control. I guess this cry had been building up for a long, long time.

"Are you okay?" I asked when she seemed calm enough to talk. At this point, we were sitting on the floor of the bathroom with our backs leaning against the radiator. Violet had a big wad of toilet paper in her hand and I was reminded of myself that day I spent half my birthday party in the bathroom. It was kind of weird not to be the one all traumatized for a change.

"It's not just missing Vermont or getting a bad social studies grade that's so horrible. *Everything's* going wrong," Violet confessed. Then she started rummaging through her backpack. "Here, I have to show you something." She pulled out a piece of paper and handed it to me. It was last week's math test with an 87% circled at the top.

"Good job," I said. I'd gotten a 73 on that test.

"It's a *B*," Violet said as though she were sharing a scandalous secret. "My parents don't know yet and I don't know how to tell them. They're going to be really upset."

I thought Violet was probably exaggerating. From what she'd told me about her parents, they seemed way too laid-back and distracted by their jobs to care one way or the other.

"Why would they be upset?"

"They expect me to be responsible about keeping up my grades."

"You're joking with me, right?" Apparently, Violet wasn't. "But you're, like, the model student. If anything, you're *too* responsible."

"What's that supposed to mean?"

"I mean, you're always so serious about everything. Your grades. Our oral report. Even medieval knights and damsels in distress. You need to loosen up. Do some goofing around. Don't you ever do dumb stuff just for fun?"

More tears formed in Violet's eyes. "I — I had fun in the Magic Castle Club," she said haltingly.

"But that was a school club. I'm talking about things that don't have anything to do with school or learning. Like hanging out with friends." I gave a little cough, recognizing that given my present friendless situation, I probably wasn't a very convincing example of someone who knew how to have fun.

"You don't know how hard I have to work to keep up my grades. It takes up a lot of time. Getting good grades is all my parents talk about."

"I thought your parents let you do your own thing and didn't tell you what to do."

"It's not like they nag me. They just expect things from me. And when I don't do well, when I screw up, they make me feel like I'm this big disappointment to them. Things are okay as long as I'm doing things that make me look smart or special. But the rest of the time they hardly notice me at all." Violet took off her glasses and wiped her eyes for about the hundredth time. "And they really want me to be a doctor like my dad."

"But isn't your dad a college professor?"

"He's a doctor who teaches other doctors. He's mostly into research, though."

"Wow." I hadn't realized that Violet's father was a professor and a doctor *and* a scientist. There I was, the first day of school, lying about my sister being a medical student while Violet was sitting there silent, not telling a soul that her father was the *ultimate* doctor.

"So, you don't want to be like your dad?" I asked, remembering the glimpse I'd had of Dr. Hayes in his rumpled shirt and messy hair.

"Being a doctor is the last thing I want to be," Violet said firmly.

"What would you rather do?"

"You'll laugh."

"No, I won't. I swear."

Violet took a deep breath.

"I want to work at a medieval fair. What I really want to

be is one of those court jesters who does all those acrobatics and tricks and stuff."

This left me speechless. I'd never been to a medieval fair, but I'd heard about them. People dress up in old-fashioned costumes and walk around selling stuff and entertaining the crowds. It was very hard for me to imagine three-facial-expression Violet doing this.

"But, Violet. To be a jester, you have to be able to *jest*," I pointed out.

"I can jest," Violet said, standing up. "And I can dance. Here, I'll show you."

She began this sort of hopping performance. Then she shook her arms and twirled around. The first thing that came to my mind was Rumpelstiltskin dancing around the fire when he thinks he's tricked the queen. If you have trouble picturing that, think of a chimpanzee having a seizure.

I didn't know if I was supposed to laugh or not, but I wanted to laugh. In fact, I wanted to laugh so much that I knew if I tried to hold it in, I would either: a) bust a blood vessel, or b) pee in my pants, so I ran into one of the stalls and howled and peed at the same time. Between howls I heard this kind of croaking noise on the other side of the door. I feared I'd hurt Violet's feelings and she was crying again.

"I'm sorry, Violet. I really am," I managed to sputter. "It's just that you looked —"

I opened the door a crack to check out Violet's condition, and there she was *laughing* at herself or at me. I don't know which.

"Is this what you mean by having fun?" she croaked.

"Yeah," I said, suddenly feeling much lighter than I'd felt in a long, long while.

MARY ANN RETURNS

Once Mrs. Lucas got around to passing out flyers about the Halloween contest to the rest of the class, talk of Angel's upcoming slumber party came to a temporary halt. Now students were talking about what costumes they would wear to school and what the prizes for the best ones would be. The contest was kind of a big deal because it was the first time in no one knew how long that middle school kids were allowed to dress up for Halloween.

Everyone held their breath, waiting for objections to be raised from ultracautious parents, the same ones who periodically pulled "inappropriate" reading material off the school library shelves and were generally suspicious of any activity that actually might be fun. But miraculously, there were no complaints about the Halloween contest that was promised to "build unity" among students. Maybe it was because the PTO, which was sponsoring the event, had come up with a ton of rules: no fake blood, no gore, nothing sexually suggestive, no weapons, which, of course, greatly limited our choices for costumes.

I have to admit that I kind of got caught up in the excitement along with everyone else. Unlike Angel's party, it was something *everyone* could participate in. If I wasn't going to be a member of a herd, I would have to rise *above* all the herds, I decided. The way I would do it would be to come up with the best costume in the sixth grade and win a really cool prize.

"Why don't you wear that cat burglar outfit you have," my dad suggested when I told my parents about the contest.

"Let Rissa come up with her own idea," my mother insisted. She'd been unusually supportive these past few days, sighing sympathetically when I told her what happened with the oral report and frowning compassionately when I told her what a rough life Violet had with her parents.

Meanwhile, Violet stopped bringing her book to lunch and we actually began having real conversations, carefully avoiding the topics of Angel's slumber party and our grades. I won't lie and say Violet and I suddenly became best friends, but after our conversation in the bathroom, we settled for a sort of truce and became more at ease with each other. Mostly, we concentrated on coming up with good ideas for costumes. Violet decided to dress up like a court jester (big surprise). I was shooting for something more dignified. Violet wanted me to be a damsel in distress, but I didn't want everyone to think we had this medieval thing going. Believe me, if there were a Magic Castle Club at the middle school, I'd be the absolute last person to join.

I had a lot of ideas for costumes, but none of them seemed quite right. They were too complicated or not original enough. I wasn't going to settle for anything as boring as a hippie, which was what Beth (along with all my ex-friends) was planning to be. On the other hand, I didn't want to be anything that involved bulky props. I'd learned my lesson about that back in third grade when I decided to be a television set. I wore this huge carton over my body and couldn't see where I was going. When I was out trick-or-treating with Beth, I tripped over a jack-o'-lantern and landed flat on my face in front of some lady's door. I couldn't get back up, so Beth had to rip open the box to save me. Then I had to go home in my underwear and T-shirt. It was pretty awful.

Anyway, Friday afternoon, I was making a list of possible costumes and remembering my past Halloweens, when Mary Ann came home. Mom and Dad were about as surprised as I was to see her car come up the drive.

"I *have* to have some peace and quiet to study for mid-terms," Mary Ann announced when she burst through the door. She was definitely "wound a little tight," as my mother would say, and *extremely* annoyed that her new roommates had turned out to be a pretty noisy, rowdy bunch, just as my parents had feared. After complaining about how self-ish they were and how unreasonable her teachers were and giving us a detailed account of what she had to do to pre-pare for her tests, she finally got around to noticing I was in the room.

"How's school going for you?" she asked with mild inter-est, and I told her about the Halloween contest.

"Why don't you go as a college student?" she suggested. "You could wear my U of I sweatshirt and carry around a bunch of books."

"I don't think so."

"Or you could be the cat in 'The Cat and the Fiddle.' You could dress up like a cat and use your violin case as a trick-or-treat bag."

"That's an interesting idea," I said politely.

Obviously, my sister had gone brain-dead from studying too hard.

Starting after dinner, my parents took Mary Ann's request for "peace and quiet" pretty seriously, and during the next two days we all got in the habit of tiptoeing around her and whispering while she was poring over her books.

Mom made me practice the violin in the basement and we all had to eat our meals in the kitchen so as not to mess up Mary Ann's papers strewn all over the dining room table.

A couple of times when Mary Ann was stationed in the dining room, I sat down at the end of the table to work on my list of ideas for costumes. She didn't seem to mind me being there as long as I didn't bug her. Seeing Mary Ann's wrinkled forehead as she highlighted sections of her book made me think of Violet.

"Have you ever heard of a Professor Hayes?" I asked her. Mary Ann looked startled.

"Zach Hayes? He was a guest lecturer for my biology class." It took me a minute to digest the fact that Dr. Hayes's first name was Zach. Somehow it didn't seem a fitting name for someone preparing the future doctors of America and trying to rid the world of disease. I went on to tell my sister about Violet, and how her parents expected her to get good grades so she could become a doctor like "Zach" someday.

"Well, you do need good grades if you want to go into medicine," Mary Ann confirmed. "But not in the sixth grade. You guys should be enjoying your childhood." Then she gave this big sigh. "I'd give *anything* to be your age again. Life was so carefree."

Obviously, my sister had missed my point about Violet being under a lot of pressure. Life was not as "carefree" for people my age as Mary Ann thought. And given the way Mary Ann started turning into a weepy teenager when she was just a couple of years older than me, you would think she would remember how awful things could get.

I promised myself that when I turned nineteen years old like my sister, I would never, ever look back and pretend my sixth grade life was easy.

❀ ❀ ❀

That weekend, when Mary Ann wasn't at the dining room table, she wandered around the house, mumbling dates and facts and formulas she was supposed to memorize. This was when she acted the most intense. I'd never seen her so serious about studying for tests in her life. She snapped at us when we did something to distract her, like, uh, cross her path to get to the bathroom. Her behavior was nerve-wracking for the rest of us, especially Mom, who had to do two duffel bags' worth of Mary Ann's laundry before she returned to school and had to keep making pots of coffee so Mary Ann could stay awake.

I think by Sunday afternoon, Mary Ann finally realized she'd been kind of a pain while she was at home or maybe she was just sick of studying, but in any case, she offered to take me out to get something to eat. Just so you know, this was not a typical thing for her to do. In fact, I think I can count the number of times on one hand that she's offered to take me somewhere. I figured something was up.

"So, where do you want to go?" Mary Ann asked as we got into her car.

"I don't know. Velvet Freeze?" I'd been afraid to ask my dad to take me there since he'd made those four smoothie trips when I was sick.

"Should we get smoothies or ice cream?"

"Ice cream."

Mary Ann put on her sunglasses, which she always wears in the car, even when it's not sunny, and we headed downtown.

At first we just made small talk. She told me about her classes, and I told her a few Mrs. Lucas stories, which made her laugh. It wasn't until we got our ice-cream cones that she got to the serious stuff. I thought whatever Mary Ann wanted to talk about had something to do with her and school. Maybe she was flunking out, or maybe she didn't have enough money for rent or something.

"So, what's up with Mom?" she asked abruptly once we'd gotten our napkins and had settled down in a booth.

"What do you mean?" I truly had no idea what she was talking about.

"You know, about the way she's acting. She's so . . . well, strange."

"Strange?"

"Yeah, strange. I mean, when I told her that I was having

some problems with my roommates, I was expecting her to say, 'I told you getting an apartment was a bad idea,' and shake her finger at me. You know how she is. But she just said, 'I'm sure things will get better, dear,' and then she patted me on the hand. Also, she didn't try to butt in to give me study tips. And she didn't bombard me with questions the way she usually does. She just left me alone all weekend. That's not like her."

It surprised me that Mary Ann, so wrapped up in her studying, even noticed how Mom had been acting that weekend, but now that I thought about it, Mary Ann was definitely onto something.

I thought back to how Mom hadn't scolded me when I told her I wasn't *absolutely* prepared for my oral report. Also, she'd given up trying to get me to make up with Beth. And there was that time in the computer room when she said she was proud of me for being independent and making a new friend. Odd. Very odd. Why hadn't I noticed this change in her sooner?

"I'm worried about her," Mary Ann confessed.

"Why?" In my mind, the change in Mom was kind of nice.

"I think she's lonely. With me being gone most of the time and you and this whole independence kick, maybe she feels like she's not useful anymore."

Mom thinking she was useless? I didn't know if I'd go that far.

Mary Ann and I were silent for a few minutes while we thought about how my mother had been acting and sucked ice cream out of the bottoms of our cones.

"And she stayed home for the entire weekend," my sister added when her ice-cream cone was almost gone. "She didn't talk on the phone or go out with Catherine White once. Aren't they friends anymore?"

Now that I thought about it, the last time I'd seen Beth's mom was when she came over with the Jell-O. I was used to Mrs. White calling or dropping by a couple of times during the week, and she and Mom almost always went someplace together on weekends. Well, they used to until a month or so ago.

"I don't know," I said in a very small voice, fearing that my separation from my old group of friends might have something to do with Mom and Mrs. White not seeing each other anymore. Until now, it hadn't occurred to me that my decision to be independent might affect my mother. But now I saw that it might. Maybe something *had* happened between Mom and Mrs. White, and it was my fault.

There was another silence as we chewed the last bites of our cones.

"Oh, well. Maybe it's nothing," Mary Ann concluded.

"Maybe Mom's just realizing we're growing up and we don't need her as much anymore."

"Of course we need her," I protested. Now I was really starting to feel sorry for my mom, who, after the birthday party, may have gotten dropped in the unpopularity pit right along with me.

Mary Ann started wiping my ice-cream drips off the table, then got up to throw away the dirty napkin and our last pieces of cone. I watched her walk to the trash can and back, wondering if I should let her in on my fears about Mom.

"Oh, I almost forgot," Mary Ann said, grabbing her purse from the table. "I brought something to show you." She fumbled around inside her purse and brought out a paperback book titled *United States Immigration Policies*, something that made Violet's books about medieval times look like easy readers.

"You want me to read this?" I asked uncertainly.

"No. Look at the picture on the cover." I glanced at the photograph of a statue.

"The Statue of Liberty?"

"Yeah. Wouldn't it make a great Halloween costume?"

At first, the idea of being the Statue of Liberty seemed about as ridiculous as being a college student or a cat burglar. I tried to picture myself wearing a long flowing gown and holding a torch high in the air. Hmm. I thought of the judges seeing me and appreciating the historic significance of my costume. I thought of how I could be a living symbol of independence. Maybe Mary Ann's idea wasn't so bad after all.

MOM'S MASTERPIECE

I told my gnomes about my conversation with Mary Ann. First I let them in on the Statue of Liberty idea. They had mixed feelings about that since they were hoping I'd be a gnome for Halloween, so I tried to explain that what I was going for was a tall, majestic look, hoping I wasn't hurting anybody's feelings. Then I asked them if they'd noticed any changes in my mom lately. Unfortunately, they didn't see her very often, so it was hard for them to tell, but Timothy said he'd always thought she was a very nice lady.

After discussing things with my gnomes, I started a campaign to be more considerate to my mother. In an effort to make her feel more useful, I asked her if she could take me to Designer's Dream, which is this store that sells every type of craft supply and fabric you could imagine. Now that I had an idea for my Halloween costume, I wanted to get going on the project right away, having learned my lesson about procrastination.

"Your costume isn't going to be anything too complicated, is it? It doesn't have anything to do with a television set, does it?" Mom asked warily when I told her I needed to buy some supplies. I assured her that all I needed was some green material, Styrofoam cones, and maybe a little face paint.

"What are you going to be? The Statue of Liberty?"

Surely she hadn't learned *this* from the mothers' network.

"How did you know?" I asked.

"Lucky guess."

Actually, she didn't seem as thrilled as I thought she'd be to take me to Designer's Dream, which was too bad. I had hoped we could sort of bond. Here we were. Two independent women in search of Halloween supplies. On the way to the mall, I chatted away about my plans for the costume, but Mom seemed kind of tired. I think the weekend with Mary Ann had worn her out.

Once we got inside the fabric store, however, Mom brightened up some. It's funny how certain stores have that effect on people. For Beth, it's Studio 99. She gets this kind of gleam in her eye the second it's within her view. Her pupils enlarge. I swear they do. It's like she wants to take in everything at once. Mary Ann has the same reaction when she visits the used bookstore next to Velvet Freeze. I guess it happens to me, too, when I go to the Rabbit Hole gift shop, which gets a new shipment of gnomes about once a month. When I'm there, I feel a million miles away from the world. My problems drift to the back of my mind. I lose track of time. You probably have a store that does the same thing to you. And I'll bet Violet Hayes has one back in Vermont. It probably sells old swords and coats of armor and jester sticks.

Anyway, my mom sort of floated through Designer's Dream with this glazed expression on her face. She seemed more interested in looking at sewing gadgets and talking to the salesclerk — someone she remembered from high school — than helping me find the stuff I needed. I managed to find the craft items on my own, but not knowing much about fabric (domestic science wouldn't start until after Christmas vacation), I had to break whatever spell Mom was under and ask her for advice.

"Mom, I need your help."

She was lovingly stroking a bolt of cloth. "But this is *your* project," she reminded me.

"It's not for a grade or anything. I *want* your help," I insisted, hoping I was making her feel useful. Mom gave in and began walking the aisles with me, rubbing various fabrics between her fingers, and stopping every now and then to pull down a bolt. Her eyes kept going back to the saleswoman, who seemed to be awfully interested in what we were doing.

We finally settled on this metallic, light green material that felt really silky, and would drape beautifully, my mother claimed. Even though the cost of it was high enough to make me gasp, Mom didn't even bat an eye when she paid for our purchases, which was really strange. And she hummed all the way home, which was even stranger since my mother is not normally a hummer.

❀ ❀ ❀

Later that night, I laid all my supplies on my bed for Nelson to admire and tried to figure how the heck I was going to make a robe out of the yards of fabric. Since I had no clue where to start, I turned my attention to the Styrofoam cones and decided I should spray-paint them first. Definitely a job to do outside on the porch.

As I passed the computer room, I looked in on my mother, who was busy working on something. There were papers lying facedown on the desk, and she was squinting at the computer screen. Her old brown sketchbook was lying on the floor by her feet.

"Mom?" She turned off the computer monitor as soon as she heard my voice. "Do you think you could help make my costume?"

She looked at me with surprise. "I'm sure you can handle it," she said. I half expected her to pat my hand.

"But I don't know how to use the sewing machine. And there aren't any rules against parents helping," I pointed out.

"I'm busy right now, but maybe tomorrow, dear." Then she shooed me off and asked me to close the door on my way out.

Closed doors? Computer work that was more important than helping me out? Mom's sketchbook out of place? Something was *definitely* up with my mom. And I thought it was something more than being lonely.

✿ ✿ ✿

The next day, my mother did what I think people call a 180-degree turn. Whereas before, she didn't seem at all interested in making my costume, now she was all gung ho. When I got home from school, she was waiting for me in the kitchen with her glue gun in hand.

"Did you still need some help with your costume?" she asked eagerly. "I've come up with a few ideas."

"Sure," I said, and I wasn't just trying to make Mom feel needed.

For the next few hours she worked steadily. First she made me a Statue of Liberty crown by gluing the spray-painted Styrofoam cones onto a thick plastic headband. Then she hauled out our old portable sewing machine from the coat closet and set it up in her bedroom.

"Okay, let me work now," she said, pushing me into the hall and closing her door.

More closed doors. What had come over her?

She was still busy sewing my costume long after my dad got home from work. He finally peeked in the bedroom and asked my mother if there were any plans for dinner, which was a polite way of asking, "Why aren't you downstairs in the kitchen cooking?" I was starting to wonder the same thing.

"I'm busy. Call out for Chinese," my mother mumbled as the sewing machine whirred. The way she worked that night reminded me of the way Mary Ann studied for her tests that past weekend. I think Dad made the connection, too, because I heard him muttering something about all the Bartholomew women turning into "fanatics."

✿ ✿ ✿

Mom was still at it when I came home from school the next day. Dad and I ate leftover Chinese food and played cards while Mom was busy putting the finishing touches on my costume.

It was almost my bedtime when she finally came downstairs, holding the robe in one hand and the flashlight torch in the other.

"I need you to try everything on," she said.

"Okay," I said eagerly.

I loved the feel of the fabric against my skin as Mom helped me slip the robe over my head. When she bobby-pinned the headpiece in place, I felt a little like Miss

America being crowned, not that I'd ever want to *be* her or anything.

"I want to see!" I said excitedly, running to the big dining room mirror. Of course I didn't *look* anything at all like a beauty queen, but I thought I *was* the spitting image of the Statue of Liberty.

"This is great! It looks really professional," I said.

"Well, I still need to hem it. Hold still so I can put in some pins," said Mom. She crouched down beside me and started tugging at the bottom of my robe.

My father wandered out of the kitchen with an apple in his hand. "Very nice! Much nicer than your cat burglar costume," he said. "I'm very impressed, Annie."

"Thanks." My mother looked pleased. "I'm kind of rusty, but I used to be pretty handy with a needle and thread."

Of course we knew this, and I thought she was going to once again tell us the story about how she won a blue ribbon for that wool suit she made. But this time she brought up a different story, one about a gown she'd made for her junior prom.

"You'd remember it, Mitch," she said dreamily. "It was a peach color with a taffeta skirt."

"Ah, yes. Of course I remember." Dad mumbled in a way that made me think he didn't.

"I'd forgotten all about that dress until I ran into my old 4-H buddy, Christine Roderick, at the fabric store. After all these years, she remembered my prom dress *and* the wool suit I made for the state fair."

Dad interrupted, saying, "I think I remember Christine from high school. Kind of a hefty girl, wasn't she?"

"Christine wasn't 'hefty.' She was — is — big-boned," Mom corrected. "And she's done very well for herself. Now she's the manager of Designer's Dream, and her store sponsors gala fashion shows both here and in Chicago."

"Maybe you could enter that wool suit of yours," Dad suggested.

"Very funny, dear." Mom pulled a loose thread from my robe. "But I did have fun making clothes." She gave me a wistful look. "Maybe I'll make something for myself, now that I have the sewing machine out."

Even though I wasn't all that interested in "Christine" or my mother's "peach taffeta prom dress," I was feeling pretty good as I listened to my parents talking. I had a terrific costume to wear to school the next day, and I was pretty sure I had succeeded in making Mom feel useful.

HALLOWEEN HORROR

I guess I don't have to tell you that my costume was a big hit at school on Halloween. I even got some envious looks from certain members of my ex-herd, who were wearing some pretty unimaginative costumes, bell-bottoms and T-shirts they'd obviously tie-dyed themselves. I wondered how many of them got in trouble for forgetting to clean out the washing machine.

Throughout the day, I got compliments. Lots and lots of compliments. Kids I didn't even know stopped me in the hallway to say how great I looked. My face was hot under the metallic green makeup, which reminded me a little of Mary Ann's gooey pimple concealer, but at least this stuff didn't cake or peel.

All in all, it was a great morning. For the first time all year, I felt glad, really glad, to be independent. If I'd stayed with my group of ex-friends, I would have been pressured to dress up as a hippie instead of something really original that stood for who I was. Feeling very patriotic and full of confidence, I kept running to the bathroom to admire myself whenever I had the chance. I wanted everything to be perfect when the judges saw me.

I felt a little bad for Violet in her jester costume. Some people just aren't cut out for wearing tights and tunics, if you know what I mean. I don't think she really cared how she looked, though. For one day she was living out her dream. So were several of the other students, I noticed. Kyle Jacobs was dressed up like Albert Einstein. Some of the boys who were into basketball wore the jerseys of their favorite Bulls players. There was your typical combination of cute and funny costumes, but my only real competition was (guess who?) Brian Bailey, who was all decked out in this really incredible knight's costume, wearing armor that was made out of aluminum pie tins, foil, and wire. I swear, Violet just about swooned when she saw him, and probably regretted not dressing up as a damsel.

It was hard for me to wait until the end of the day when there was a special assembly to announce the winners of the contest. Time seemed to move so slowly. If the novelty of wearing Halloween costumes to school wore off for some students, it didn't for me. I was at the front of the line when we trooped down to the auditorium.

Once all the students were settled, the PTO president

gave a little speech about how pleased she was that all the costumes were so original and tasteful. (Translation: Nobody wore fake blood or showed too much skin.) Those who knew they didn't have a chance for a prize stopped listening after a few seconds. Only a few of us hopefuls stayed alert. The panel of judges was introduced and there was a polite round of applause. Then the winners from each grade were announced.

I can't remember who the seventh and eighth grade winners were. All I remember is hearing the word "tie" for the sixth grade division right before my name and Brian Bailey's name were given.

It wasn't until both of us were making our way to the stage, quite pleased with ourselves, that someone (whose voice sounded an awful lot like Angel's) yelled, "Rissa Bartholomew and her knight in shining armor!!!!!" That's when the joke clicked with me. I don't know if Brian got it or not, but all the taunts I'd received since the playground incident came flooding back, and the audience (at least the sixth graders) seemed to remember it, too.

Someone whistled. Quite a few people laughed. The rest of what happened was your typical nightmare scene. As soon as we got onstage, Brian and I were met with a chorus of kissing noises. There were also a few "woo-hoos."

Trying to remain as dignified as possible as the Statue of Liberty, I graciously accepted my award, a gift certificate to Dino's Pizzeria. My heart sank. The jeers continued. The PTO president didn't seem to hear the kissing sounds and shouts, or maybe she just chose to ignore them. In any case, she leaned in close to the microphone and said, "Let's give these students a big hand." There was a thunderous response that included the stamping of feet.

"Hey, Brian, give the Statue of Liberty a kiss!!!"

I could have died.

Brian opened his aluminum-foil helmet and sort of tipped toward me, and for one horrible moment, I thought that he *was* going to try to give me a kiss. In reflex, I stuck out my torch and poked him in the stomach, much harder than I meant to. It must have been the adrenaline.

Stunned, Brian flailed his arms. It all seemed to be happening in slow motion. He teetered at the edge of the stage, losing his balance. He emitted a low-pitched "ooooooh," then as the audience gasped, he fell into the pit. It was not a graceful fall. His limbs jerked. His body twisted, and he landed in an awkward position dangerously close to the first row of seats. There were a few screams from the audience, then a beat of silence, as though everyone in the auditorium was drawing a breath at the same time. Then I heard the PTO president say, "Oh, my Lord!" and our principal, Mr. Shraeder, jumped to his feet and ran down the aisle to the pit, shouting to no one in particular, "We need an ambulance!"

CHAPTER 23

CRIME AND PUNISHMENT

While Brian (who was not killed, by the way) was being rushed to the hospital, I was sitting in the office awaiting the principal and — worse than that — my mother, who had been notified of the accident directly after Mrs. Bailey was called. I wondered what the punishment for causing a student to fall off the stage would be. I figured it would be something more than a stern lecture.

I was thankful that school already had been dismissed for the day by the time Mr. Shraeder appeared and I heard my mother's heels *click, click, click*ing down the corridor. I'm not sure what exactly they told her on the phone, but she seemed bewildered and very, very concerned when she walked into the principal's office. I must have looked terrified because the first thing she did was to give me a hug.

"What exactly happened?" she asked anxiously, turning her head back and forth between me and Mr. Shraeder.

"Clarissa was responsible for a very serious injury," my principal said in a grave tone. He went on to explain his version of Brian's accident.

All the while, Mom looked at me questioningly. I wanted to tell her everything, how it wasn't my fault, how I didn't mean to hurt Brian, but instead I just burst into tears.

To sum up a horrid and depressing story, I got off with a two-day suspension. The school got off with having to pay for Brian's hospital bills. And my mother left the office furious with Mr. Shraeder, not me.

It wasn't until we were safely in the car that I told Mom my own shortened version of what happened. I have to admit that I did leave out some parts. I just couldn't bring myself to tell her that I was afraid that Brian was going to kiss me, so I said I knocked him with the flashlight by accident. I know it was sort of a lie, but there was no way — and I hope that you believe me — that I meant for him to fall and hurt himself.

Mom (unlike my principal) accepted what I told her with a nod, assuring me all along that she *knew* it had to have been an accident, which was yet another example of her not acting like herself. I mean, I could think of a lot of words to describe the mom I *used* to know — nosy, bossy, tidy, in-the-know, penny-pinching — but "understanding" would definitely not be on the list.

I mean, of course, my mother was upset that Brian was hurt, but at the same time, she seemed just as concerned with how I was feeling about the whole ordeal, especially the part about being suspended. I wasn't used to her asking how I felt. Always before, Mom's motto was "Yell first, ask questions later." This time, there was no yelling at all.

I guess it was partly because of the way my mom acted so gentle and all that I felt so horribly guilty. I had realized by then that Brian probably had no intention of kissing me. It was really dumb of me to think that he — or anyone for that matter — would do something like that in public with teachers watching and everything. I wished that there was some way I could let him know about the terrible mistake I'd made, but what would I say? "The idea of you kissing me was so repulsive that I felt I had to protect myself"? I wished I could just erase Halloween, or better yet, erase the whole school year so far.

As soon as we got home, Mom called Brian's house to see how he was. When there was no answer, she tried the hospital. The nurse there wasn't allowed to tell her anything, but she did connect my mother with Brian's mother.

Immediately, my mother started gushing with apologies.

"And how is Brian doing?" she finally got around to asking. I sort of wanted to know the answer and I sort of didn't want to know. I closed my eyes tight but left my ears open.

"Oh, dear! . . . Oh, *dear*! Well, we want you to know that Rissa feels just horrible. She'd like to apologize to Brian, herself, of course. Is he able to come to the phone?"

What? My eyes snapped open.

"I see. Well, perhaps Rissa could talk to you, and you could give him the message." My heart started beating wildly as my mother handed me the phone.

"Hello, Mrs. Bailey?" I said shakily.

"Hello, dear."

"I'm sorry for what happened."

"The important thing is that Brian's going to be all right. I'm sure you didn't mean to hurt him." Mrs. Bailey's voice was soft and soothing.

Fearing that I'd burst into tears for a second time that afternoon, I couldn't bring myself to ask how badly Brian had been hurt. I had to wait and find out from Mom that he'd broken his foot.

That night, I didn't feel much like celebrating Halloween. I couldn't have gone trick-or-treating anyway, not because my mother wouldn't let me, but because the second I got home from school I dumped my costume *and* the gift certificate to Dino's Pizzeria into the garbage can.

Mom and I ate a quiet dinner alone. Dad had to work

late. He was meeting with one of his advertising clients, the Pampered Lawn Service guy, who (unfortunately for the rest of the world) liked to make up his own commercials and insisted on acting in them, singing this really stupid "This Lawn Is Our Lawn" jingle to the tune of "This Land Is Your Land."

Usually, I hated it when Dad had to work extra hours drumming up advertising business for his station, but that evening I was glad he wasn't home. Chances were that he wouldn't be quite so calm as Mom was when he found out I got suspended. Don't get me wrong. He's usually pretty easygoing and hardly ever loses his temper over little things, but when something really big happens (like one of his children getting a suspension that would go on their permanent record), he tends to sort of blow up. I hoped I'd be asleep by the time that happened.

Since I had nothing better to do after dinner, I stationed myself in the living room to pass out candy (usually Dad's job) to trick-or-treaters, figuring it might cheer me up to see some of the cute little kids in the neighborhood all dressed up as princesses and bunnies. It was kind of fun at first, but as it got later, the people ringing the bell were not so cute and little. When one rather large ghost asked, "Hey, aren't you that girl who knocked that boy off the stage?" I knew it was time to let my mom start answering the door.

Soon after that, I went to bed, but I couldn't get to sleep. I was still awake when Dad came in, and I held my breath, anticipating the worst. I heard my parents talking, but there was no sound of my father hitting the ceiling. Either my mother didn't tell him what happened, or he was too tired to be upset.

I think that maybe I would have felt better if Dad had come upstairs to bawl me out or at least acknowledge the fact that I'd done something really stupid. I felt so alone, being the only one who knew the whole truth about the accident (meaning *why* I poked Brian). I kept thinking about Brian and wondered how much worse it might feel to get poked in the stomach and fall off a stage than to have an allergic reaction to tomatoes or to sprain an ankle on the playground, which were the most serious ailments I'd ever suffered. Let's see. On a scale of ten, if getting hives and twisting my ankle were 8's, I figured a sharp blow beneath the ribs followed by a blind back dive off the stage would rank about a 14.

I tried to put myself in Brian's shoes. What would my first reaction be if someone hit me for no reason? Would I be shocked? Confused? Scared? In major pain? All of the above? Definitely. And I'd probably think the person who threw the punch hated my guts.

Maybe worse than breaking Brian's foot (which I realize

is pretty serious) was the fact that now he'd think that I was just the same as all the other tormentors who'd made his life miserable over the years. The whole reason I'd left the herd in the first place was to protect Brian from getting embarrassed, and look what happened. I think this is what Mrs. Lucas would call one of those cases of irony.

I kept picturing Brian lying in a hospital bed, baffled and in terrible pain. Then I remembered his face as he was losing his balance and heard the "ooooh" that escaped when he toppled over. What a humiliating thing to have happen to a person. He must have felt like a real dork. Some people deserved to feel like dorks, but Brian did not. He didn't have a mean bone in his body. Just a broken one.

I had a long heart-to-heart talk with Nelson about what I had done, but he just stared at me blankly and didn't have any advice to give for once. I knew I had to tell someone else, so I went downstairs to my parents.

I almost hated to wreck the peaceful scene of Mom and Dad at the kitchen table. Dad was eating some leftovers from a Tupperware bowl. Mom was filling out some form, which she quickly flipped over when I came in the room. I wondered if it had something to do with my suspension.

"Can't sleep?" Mom asked. I shook my head.

"I need to talk to you about something." I took a deep breath, then I told them the complete story, including *why* I hit Brian with my torch.

"Atta girl!" my dad said, raising his fist in the air. "Now all the boys in your school know not to mess with Rissa Bartholomew!" He obviously thought my poking Brian was some kind of brilliant self-defense maneuver.

"I don't believe Brian was attempting to 'mess' with your daughter," my mother said. Then she cleared her throat and suggested we go up to my room.

It's not like my bad feelings about myself suddenly disappeared or anything after my confession. But I did feel less alone and safer when my mother tucked me in bed the way she did when I was little.

"It seems to me that this is all a matter of a big misunderstanding," she said, smoothing my covers. "I just wish that principal of yours understood that instead of worrying so much about the school getting sued. I've never liked that man much."

This was the first time I'd ever heard my mother say something against a school employee. She even stuck up for the custodian who made kids clean out toilets when they were too rowdy in the halls. I must have looked shocked because Mom told me not to worry so much.

"These things happen," she said. "It's too bad, but they happen."

"Well, I wish it hadn't happened to me."

Mom nodded and sat down beside me.

"They happen to everyone, Rissa. Especially to the hot-tempered women on my side of the family. I remember one time in high school, someone sneaked up behind me and grabbed me around the waist. I swung around and belted him right in the face. Really hard. So hard I broke his nose."

"Really?" I gasped. "Who was it?"

"Your father."

I should have known.

MY SUSPENSION

Here is a list of the things I worried about during my two-day suspension:

★ 1. That Brian thought I was mean and hated him.

★ 2. That Brian would never fully regain the use of his leg (I watched a lot of soap operas during my suspension).

★ 3. That I would not be able to make up the schoolwork I missed.

★ 4. That I had lost Mrs. Lucas's respect by causing injury to one of her students.

★ 5. That everyone would think that Brian was an even bigger dork after the accident.

★ 6. That my parents (who were acting way too nice) were secretly plotting some horrible punishment that they might spring on me at any moment.

Here is a list of things I did to distract myself from worrying:

★ 1. Talked to my gnomes.

★ 2. Watched soap operas (I think I already mentioned that).

★ 3. Watched Mom make a velour tracksuit for herself (she's really on this sewing kick now).

★ 4. Avoided answering the phone in case it was someone who had heard about Brian's fall.

★ 5. Practiced "Peanut Butter Cookie" and "Twinkle, Twinkle, Little Star," another song I've learned, on the violin.

★ 6. Wrote a letter to Brian that I will never send, and this is what it said:

Dear Brian,

I am really, really, hoping that you can forgive me for ~~pushing you~~ accidentally causing you to fall off the school stage and suffer a serious injury. I just want you to know that I believe there are many students at Hickory Grove Middle School who deserve to have their feet broken, but you are not one of them. You are one of the most kindhearted people in the world and not the least bit dorky. And I really appreciated it that time in fourth grade when I fell on the playground (suffering a less serious injury than you are suffering now), and you helped me to the nurse's office. Perhaps you should consider a career in medicine. You are really good at making people feel better. In any case, I hope you have a speedy recovery.

Yours truly,

Rissa Bartholomew

P.S. Please remember to keep your feet elevated. Terence Davenport, this character on a soap opera I watch, forgot to put his feet up after breaking his leg and died from a blood clot.

DARK NOVEMBER

I think it would be safe to say that the absolute darkest period of sixth grade came when I returned to school after my suspension. That first Monday back was the worst. I'm not going to tell you every detail about what happened because, to be honest, there's quite a lot I'd like to forget, but to give you an idea of what went on, here are some of the high- (or should I say *low*-) lights:

When I arrived a half hour early as instructed, I was taken into the counselor's office. This was so Mrs. Stevenson, my assigned counselor (whom I'd only met once), could give me a little talk on anger management and "striking out" at others. I probably should have listened, because I do have what my mother calls a "short fuse," but the thing was, I didn't hit Brian because I was mad at him. I was mad at the audience. It's just that Brian was in the way. Anyway, the whole experience with Mrs. Stevenson was just too embarrassing for words. I sat in silence, stroking Nicholas's head, and got out of there as soon as I could. Then I slunk to my locker, where someone had written the words *Psycho Girl* in permanent marker.

I was standing there beside my locker, staring at the words, wondering who could have written them, when Brian came hobbling down the hall on crutches. He was followed by a group of sympathetic girls, who were asking to sign his cast. I guess he'd missed a couple of days of school, too. I knew I should go up to him and apologize, but that would have been pretty impossible with all those people around. There was one really uncomfortable moment when Brian looked over at me. He blushed and I'm sure I did, too. For the rest of the day, we took pains not to make eye contact.

After about the first hour of school, it became very clear that while I was gone serving my suspension, the sixth graders had divided themselves into three groups:

★ 1. Those who believed that I was some kind of nutcase (like the person who wrote on my locker).

★ 2. Those who believed Brian was a tragic victim (like the girls who wanted to sign his cast).

★ 3. Those who thought the whole incident between Brian and me was this huge joke (like most of the soccer boys).

Some students fell into more than one category.

❀　❀　❀

I have to give Violet credit for showing some loyalty to me that day (although I suspected that she shared some of the concerns as the kids in group number 1). She did walk with me to the cafeteria, but she didn't walk quite as close as she usually did. Maybe snapping at her wasn't the right approach to convince her that I wasn't "psycho."

"What is your problem?" I asked crossly.

"Nothing," she said meekly, taking a giant step backward as though she expected me to take a swing at her.

"You're acting like you're scared of me."

"No, I'm not."

"Yes, you are. Don't you get it, Violet? What happened in the auditorium was a misunderstanding," I said, quoting my mother. "I didn't mean to hurt Brian. I just poked him. I didn't know he'd fall off the stage."

"I don't know, Rissa. It looked like a pretty big whack from where I was sitting."

"Just trust me. I had my reasons." I didn't say what the reasons were.

"It's just that . . . I never thought of you as a violent type of person before."

"It was a onetime thing, okay?" I was starting to get exasperated.

"Okay." Violet took a hesitant step closer to me.

"We're friends, right? I really need you to be on my side."

"I'm on your side," said Violet. But I wish she sounded more definite about it.

"What have people been saying about me?" I asked in a whisper. "Do most of the kids think that I pushed Brian off the stage on purpose?"

From the way Violet kind of danced around the question, not giving me a straight answer, I could tell there had been a lot of discussion on the subject.

❀ ❀ ❀

The rest of the week was only slightly better than that first day. I'd definitely made a name for myself in the sixth grade, and it was not a good name. I remembered back to the beginning of the school year when I longed for someone to notice me. Now I wished people *wouldn't* notice me quite so much. In fact, there were times — many times — that I wished I were invisible.

I guess the incident might not have been such a big deal if I'd gone to a bigger school where stuff like kids falling off the stage is always going on, but Hickory Grove Middle School is a pretty low-key place. And parents like it that way. I mean, families move here *because* of the "stable" school system. There aren't fistfights in the halls or bomb threats or gangs. When kids want to hurt people around here, they use words instead of blows.

I longed for Beth, Angel, Kerry, and Jayne to walk me down the hall like they had that day when I had hives. I wanted Beth to give me a hug and tell me everything was going to be okay. I wanted to see Angel shrug her shoulders and say pushing Brian off the stage was no big deal. And I wanted to hear Kerry and Jayne tell me how mean and unfair Mr. Shraeder was for giving me a suspension. But things were different now. And it was even worse than getting snubbed. It was like my ex-friends were walking on eggshells, waiting for me to blow any second. Everybody was. And there was no stopping the spread of gossip.

The most hurtful comment that I overheard about the "incident" came from Skimpy-top girl number 1, whose name was Alexandra. When she was standing at the drinking fountain with Skimpy-top girl number 2 (Cassandra), she said, "I always thought that Rissa girl was kind of strange, but what she did to Brian was just plain cruel."

Cruel? Being called that was worse than being called psycho. Don't ever believe what they tell you about sticks and stones.

It took Violet until Wednesday to relax around me again, and then things were okay at lunch at least. To be fair, she did make some effort to cheer me up, mostly by recounting how Celia put up a brave front when some of the villagers turned against her. But Violet had a lot to learn about how to make a friend feel better and how to protect her from harsh words and how to build up her confidence.

Since no one was willing to set the world straight and declare that I was a decent, horribly misunderstood person, I had to take care of myself. I had to watch every word I said and every gesture I made to prove to everyone else that I was not some kind of crazy bully. I smiled at people so much my face hurt, and I tried to be extra helpful and considerate, picking up pencils that were dropped in the aisle, complimenting girls on their clothes, and congratulating the soccer players when I heard they'd won a game. I studied extra hard, hoping to win back Mrs. Lucas's respect, and I made a point of always saying hello to our principal even though the very sight of him made my stomach flip.

It was exhausting work. And sometimes I doubted that I was making any progress at all.

As the week dragged on, I couldn't help wondering what was going on inside Beth's mind when I caught her staring at me. She'd known me longer than anyone else in the sixth grade. I didn't think it could be possible that *she'd* believe I'd hurt Brian on purpose, but everyone was acting so strangely, it was hard to really know.

I did notice that she appeared to be one of those girls who viewed Brian as a tragic victim. She even helped him with his crutches one time when he had to get out of his seat for something. That made me want to run up to Brian and say, "This girl is a fake. She's said about a million mean things about you behind your back. And *I'm* the one who's always stuck up for you." But seeing as I was avoiding looking at, much less speaking to, Brian, that would have been kind of a hard thing to do.

Almost every day, I swore to myself that I'd call Brian after school and tell him I was sorry, but when I got home, I always chickened out. I felt like such a coward and sometimes I almost believed that maybe there *was* something wrong with me.

During this time, I think Mom noticed how down I was because she went out of her way to be nice to me. She did little things to make me feel better, like sitting down with me when I did my homework and rewarding me with ice cream when I was done. She even offered to take me to the video store one afternoon. And she always made a point of being around when I came home from school. I started to think she was the only person in the world who understood what I was going through, which is really weird because I used to think that my dad was the one who knew me best.

When Friday finally came, I had never been so relieved

for a week to be over. As I left the building, I was surprised to see Mom's car parked in front of the school. Given the way things had been going, I assumed the worst and was fearful there had been some family emergency. But when I opened the door, Mom was smiling. She was also all dressed up, I noticed.

As I slid into the seat, she said, "I thought we could go to the mall to get you a recital dress," like it was something we were in the habit of doing all the time.

"A recital dress?" I repeated dumbly. Was she talking about a *new* one? Not some designer one that was no doubt hanging in Beth's closet waiting to be handed down to me?

"I need to go to the fabric store, anyway, so this way we can kill two birds with one stone."

"You mean go to the mall right now, before I practice violin or anything?"

"You can practice later."

I didn't protest. But I did think my mother was a little overdressed for the occasion. On the other hand, she didn't get out much.

CHAPTER 26

CONFESSIONS AT THE MALL

Mom seemed a little nervous once we got to Southfield Shopping Center, and I wondered if she was regretting her decision to buy me a dress when Beth probably had several too-small ones that would fit me just fine. Or maybe Mom was planning to give me some sappy lecture on how things were bound to get better in middle school. I hoped that wasn't the case. I just wanted her to keep being nice to me. I didn't want to have a big emotional talk.

She decided to stop by the food court for coffee before we started shopping, which was kind of odd since she was acting so jumpy already. Not only did she buy herself a *large* coffee, she bought me a hot pretzel, and suggested that we sit down at a table in front of the pretzel stand instead of getting right down to the business of buying me something new.

While we were sitting, she took out her compact and

looked at herself in the mirror. Then she fished around in her purse for her eyeliner, which she applied with great care.

"What are you getting at the fabric store?" I asked, wondering if she was expecting to run into someone more important than her friend Christine.

"I'm not getting anything. I'm dropping something off. . . ." Mom looked into her coffee cup. "Can you keep a secret?"

Mom was letting me in on a secret? This got my attention. I leaned in closer and told her I *could* keep a secret.

"I'm applying for a job," she whispered.

I held my pretzel in midair, unable to take a bite, unable to put it down. A *job*? First I felt stunned, then a little angry, like maybe she was bribing me with a dress to soften the blow of abandoning me for some career.

"What kind of job?" I asked.

"Assistant manager at Designer's Dream. Christine told me there was an opening and encouraged me to apply. She gave me some forms to fill out." Mom pulled some papers out of her purse. "I wanted to check it out with you first," she confided. "It would mean there would be some changes for you."

Like I hadn't experienced about a million changes already.

"What would you be doing?"

"Mostly helping customers and working the register at first."

Mom paused to take another swig of coffee and wait for my approval, which didn't come right away. It was hard for me to imagine my mother, the last stay-at-home mom in America (except for Mrs. White), wanting to get a job. It was even harder for me to imagine myself coming home every day to an empty house. I'm sure I must have looked flustered. It was taking a while to absorb everything Mom said. I just couldn't picture her on the other side of a cash register. Wasn't working as a cashier the type of job high school kids and retired people took?

"Why do you want to go back to work now?" I asked.

"For a lot of reasons, I guess. Partly for the money. I hate how we're always having to pinch pennies, and I know how you hate having to wear Beth's hand-me-downs."

I felt a wave of guilt remembering the fuss I made last time Mrs. White brought over a box of clothes and how I'd "ruined" them by dyeing them black.

"Watching you trying out new things this year has started me thinking that I need to get out of my rut," she said, quickly adding, "Not that I don't love being a mom, of course."

"That's great," I said, but actually my feelings were still mixed. Of course, I didn't know if she'd get the job or not. And I didn't know how many hours she'd be at work if she did get it. Still, I had a sinking feeling that no matter what happened, I'd soon be spending even more time by myself than I already was.

"You don't look all that happy," Mom noticed.

"No, really. I hope that you get the job." I was thinking that I should have worked harder to make Mom feel more useful at home. Maybe Mary Ann was right about her believing we didn't need her anymore.

"Thanks, Rissa. It's just that I've been feeling this urge to do something on my own for a change. What I'd really like to do is to get some retail experience, then open a little boutique of my own someday where I could sell some of my designs. What do you think?"

I thought it sounded an awful lot like my mom was declaring her independence, and I just hoped she knew what she was in for.

We went to Designer's Dream first, and I waited outside while Mom dropped off her application. While she was talking to her friend Christine, I tried to imagine her waiting on customers. How would she handle noisy groups of kids who messed up her displays? Would she yell and chase after them like the shoe salesman at Step Ahead, or would she be more like the gray-haired cashier at Velvet Freeze, who was always messing up orders? I hoped that people would be kind to my mother if she made mistakes.

One thing was for sure, though. Her days would be a lot different than they were now, and so would mine. I wondered if Mom's mind would always be on work. Would she still have time left to worry about how I was getting along, and whether I was still "feuding" with Beth, and how Violet was "adjusting" to Illinois? Would she still do little things to make me feel better when I was down?

By the time Mom left the store, I'd kind of lost interest in finding a recital dress and told her we didn't have to go shopping if she needed to go home and recuperate from applying for a job.

"But I don't want to go home," she insisted, sounding far more energetic than I felt. "I'm in a dress-shopping mood."

So we took off in the direction of Goldstein's department store, bypassing Studio 99 on the way.

I hadn't had a whole lot of experience buying dresses, so I didn't realize what a chore it would be to find a halfway decent one. If you're around my age, you probably already know what it's like. Most of the stores you want to go to don't even sell dresses, and the stores your mother wants to go to do sell dresses, but they all look like something you'd wear to a wedding — if you happened to be the flower girl.

The dresses in the girls' department were all too little-kiddish, full of ruffles, bows, and pin-on flowers, so we tried the junior department. After I'd tried on a few foo-foo dresses — some clingy ones and others with big, full skirts — my mother agreed that none of them were right. When I came out of the dressing room wearing this one strapless dress with built-in bra cups that I'd *never* come close to filling, my mother became absolutely convinced that a dress from the junior department wasn't the answer, either.

"Maybe we should try some of the shops downtown," she suggested.

"Maybe I could just wear a skirt and top," I answered, remembering some soft-looking sweaters I'd seen in the window of Studio 99.

"Wouldn't that be too casual?" Mom said, worried. "I thought Mr. Keesly told your father that you were supposed to get dressed up."

I took another look at the bridesmaidish-type dresses and imagined what I'd look like in some of them, playing "Peanut Butter Cookie."

"What if I wore a really *nice* top and a *dressy* skirt?" I asked.

"Hm, that might work," Mom agreed, so we began our search for a skirt that wasn't too long or short and didn't have slits up the side. It was a long search, and I was about ready to give up when the obvious solution finally dawned on me.

"You could make me a skirt!" I said. The idea seemed good for a couple of reasons. For one thing, we'd save money, and there might be enough left over for a Studio 99 sweater. Also, if Mom got all involved in a project, maybe she'd change her mind about wanting to get a job.

"Are you sure you wouldn't mind wearing something handmade?"

I shook my head, but still felt a tiny twinge of doubt. "Would it be okay if I picked out the fabric and helped design it?" I asked hopefully.

"You weren't thinking of dressing all in black, were you?"

"No, I was thinking light blue."

"Well, then. I'd love it if we worked together," she said, sounding relieved.

Then she started to hum.

We took off toward the escalator, and I figured I'd better ask my second question while Mom was still in an agreeable mood.

"And could I also get a sweater from Studio 99?"

My mother stopped humming and looked at me questioningly. "Studio 99? Isn't that a very *expensive* store for older girls?"

"Sort of. But there were these sweaters in the window —"

Mom knew exactly which ones I meant. She'd seen them, too.

"They were nice," she admitted. "Your taste is getting very grown up."

"I *am* in middle school, now," I reminded her.

"So you are," Mom sighed.

While we were standing in line at Studio 99 waiting to buy my new blue sweater and — *get this* — a couple of bras that were on sale, I was beginning to think that maybe it wouldn't be so bad if my mom went back to work after all. I could get into the part about having more money to buy new clothes.

I was dreaming about the kind of skirt I wanted Mom to make when I saw two people come into the store whom I totally did not want to see, and all of a sudden, my nice, content moment was gone.

"Catherine!" My mom saw them, too.

"Annie!" Mrs. White rushed over and air-kissed Mom. Beth came over at a slower pace.

"I've been meaning to call you," Mrs. White said.

"Me too." They stood there grinning at each other in silence while Beth and I stayed rooted behind our respective mothers. Finally, my mom said, "We're here getting some new clothes for Rissa to wear to her violin recital."

"Really! When is that going to be?" Oh, no. Mrs. White was getting out her appointment book. She wasn't planning to come, was she? It was true that Mom and I had attended every dance recital Beth ever had, but it certainly wasn't necessary for them to pay us back.

"It's no big deal," I interrupted.

"Of course it's a big deal." Mom put her arm around me and for a moment I was afraid she was going to put her hand over my mouth.

The person in line in front of us walked away with an armload of bags, and it was our turn at the register. Beth and her mother watched intently as my new bras were carefully folded and bagged, a process that seemed to take about an hour.

"We're here to get Bethany some socks," Mrs. White explained once our purchase was completed. "Rissa, why don't you help her pick some out while your mother and I chat?"

I had no choice but to follow Beth to the sock section at the back of the store. We stood several feet apart and stared at the assortment of socks.

"These are cute," I said, pointing to some hideous fuzzy orange ones.

Beth smiled but didn't look at me. She remained focused on the rack nearest to her. I mean, really, how much concentration does it take to decide on a new pair of socks?

"My mom's thinking about going back to work," I said, breaking the uncomfortable silence.

"Really? What's she going to do?"

"Maybe work at Designer's Dream."

"That's nice, you'd probably get a discount on crafts."

I hadn't thought of that.

"No, really," Beth turned to look at me. "It's cool that your mom's getting a job. Designer's Dream would be perfect for her. She knows so much about sewing and everything. Remember that great Cinderella dress she made?"

"Yeah."

There was another beat of silence, then Beth cleared her throat. "I've been wanting to talk to you," she said.

"What about?" I didn't like the seriousness of her voice and hoped whatever she wanted to say didn't have anything to do with Brian Bailey's "accident."

"I know some kids are saying some not-so-nice things about you at school."

"Thanks for reminding me."

"No, I mean that's not what I wanted to tell you. I just wanted you to know that I haven't been saying anything mean. I don't know what exactly happened up there onstage, but I do know that you must have had a good reason to push Brian."

"I didn't push him. I poked him."

"Whatever." Beth flipped through a row of polka-dot socks. "Did Brian say something to make you mad or something?"

"No. The whole thing was an accident. I feel horrible about it."

"Does *he* know that?"

"I hope so."

"Did you talk to him about it?"

"Not exactly, but I apologized to his mother."

"That's not any good, Rissa," Beth said, now giving me her full attention. "Kids always have to say they're sorry to grown-ups whether they mean it or not. You really, really need to talk to Brian. You can't let the whole year go by with him and everyone else at school wondering why you pushed him off the stage."

"I didn't *push* him," I repeated, wondering what kind of discussions she and Brian had been having behind my back. I'd noticed that they'd been getting kind of chummy lately, with her helping him with his crutches and all. "Can *you* tell Brian I'm sorry?" I asked.

"Nuh-uh. You need to do it yourself."

It was hard for me to admit it, but I knew Beth was right.

"Well, maybe I *will* talk to him. And thanks for believing I didn't hurt Brian on purpose," I said. "It was a kind of complicated situation."

"Yeah, it seems like a lot of things are getting complicated this year," Beth said thoughtfully.

"Is everything going okay with you?"

"Yes. No. Sort of." I knew Beth well enough to realize something more than Brian's fall was bothering her.

"Did something happen between you and Jayne?"

Beth shook her head.

"A boy?"

"I wish," Beth sighed.

"Are your parents driving you nuts?"

"Yeah, but that's nothing new." I wondered how long Beth was going to make me go on with this guessing game.

"So, how was Angel's slumber party?"

"The party?" Beth turned a little pale, and I knew I'd hit on something. "Why? What did you hear about it?"

"Nothing."

"Oh, Rissa, it was awful." Beth took a step closer to me. "It turned out to be one of those make-out parties. Some kids were really getting into it, but I just wanted to go home."

"So, I guess you didn't 'make out' with anyone," I said in an innocent voice, and Beth shot me a dirty look.

Then she lowered her voice to tell me more about the party. "Angel swiped some beer from upstairs, and some of the kids were taking drinks of it." She paused, waiting for me to look shocked, I think. "Everybody was trying to get Jayne and me to take some, too, but we wouldn't. I was desperate to get out of there, so I called my mom on my cell phone, and Jayne and I left early. That made Angel mad, and everyone else thinks we're prudes."

"I don't think you're a prude," I said. "I would have left the party, too."

Beth pulled down a pair of plain, pink socks — the ones I knew she was going to choose — and considered a pair of navy blue ones.

"Sometimes I wish I could be little again. I really miss . . ."

Was she going to say she missed me? I held my breath waiting, but she didn't finish the sentence.

"Hey, Beth? You and your mom really, really don't need to come to my recital if you don't want to," I told her.

"No, I want to come. You've been to all of mine."

"It's not like I'm any good at violin or anything."

"I don't care. That's not why I'd come. It's just what friends do for each other, you know?" She turned away, embarrassed to mention the F word, I guess. I probably should have let it go, but I just couldn't.

"So, you mean you still think of me as a friend even though I'm not in the group anymore?" I could tell Beth wasn't sure what to say.

"Well, you're really tight with Violet, and Jayne is my best friend now," she finally admitted, and I felt a pang of jealousy. "But you and I have a history, you know? I guess I'll always think of you as a friend. My *oldest* friend. How about you? Do you still think of me as your friend?"

I thought carefully before answering. "Sometimes you make me really mad," I confessed. "But other times I really miss doing stuff with you." I didn't realize how much until that second.

"How come you never call me anymore?" Beth asked, and I just shrugged. She could have just as easily called me.

I was about to suggest that maybe we could do something sometime, but just then, we heard our mothers' voices coming from the front of the store. They were still standing near the cashier, and they appeared to be in an argument over something. Beth and I looked at each other, then took a few steps closer to see what was going on.

Mrs. White was pushing a business card at my mother. My mother was pushing it back, saying that Mrs. White would be better off if she didn't listen to idle gossip.

"Sometimes it takes a friend to point out what's happening right in front of your nose," Mrs. White said, waving the card in the air. "There's nothing shameful about seeking outside help for your child." Customers swerved their heads to see whose child needed to seek help.

My mouth dropped open.

They were talking about me!

"Quick, let's leave here before people realize they belong to us." Beth grabbed my hand, and we sneaked past our mothers to get out of the store unnoticed.

While Beth and I sat in the food court, trying to catch our breath, I had the eeriest feeling that I'd experienced this moment before. Not because I was at the same table where Mom and I had our "talk," but because what just happened at Studio 99 sort of reminded me of what happened between me and my ex-friends at my birthday party. Only this time, it was our mothers making a scene, and Beth and I (along with about twenty other shoppers) were the onlookers.

"Can you believe them?" Beth moaned. "I could have died!"

"How do you think *I* felt? They were talking about me!" We sat in irritated silence. Then something deeper and more painful than annoyance started gnawing at my stomach as I remembered what Mrs. White had said to my mother.

"What did your mom mean about me needing 'outside help'?" I asked Beth.

"You don't want to know," she said, but she told me anyway.

"Do you remember back at our birthday party when you went to the bathroom?" (Like I could forget.) "While you were gone, my mother said something to your mom about your moodiness and how she thought you should see a therapist."

I gasped, horrified that Mrs. White might think I needed *that* kind of help.

"Don't feel bad, Rissa," Beth said, putting her hand on my arm. "My mother thinks *everyone* should see a therapist. Heck, she and Dad have been seeing one for as long as I can remember."

"Really?" This was a piece of gossip that my mom hadn't let slip.

"Anyway, your mother blew up at my mom. You should have seen her. She really told my mother off and stuck up for you and everything. And the rest of us just sat there not knowing what to do or say. The party kind of fizzled out after that." Beth shifted her glance away from me. "At first I blamed you for wrecking the party, but I guess it was more our mothers' fault than yours."

"My mom stuck up for me?"

Beth nodded her head.

It had never occurred to me that something so dramatic was going on while I was in the bathroom of Dino's. I figured that everyone just sat around talking about how much they hated me. It was so weird to think that at the very same time I was on the toilet reading graffiti and thinking about Amber T., my mom was battling it out with Mrs. White. It was kind of like she was Violet's knight with the silver sword, fighting valiantly for my honor, and I was Princess Celia hiding in the woods.

"Were our mothers fighting, I mean talking, about the same subject today?" I asked, trying not to appear too anxious.

"Yeah. I think my mom was trying to give your mom the number of her therapist."

"She *still* thinks I need to get help?" I felt heat rush to my face.

"She heard what happened in the auditorium with you and Brian, but you know how things get twisted. I tried to set her straight and tell her that you didn't actually *attack* Brian the way people were saying. . . ."

I sat in stunned silence, fixated on the idea that Mrs. White not only thought I was "moody," but also thought I was some kind of monster who went around attacking people. Was the news that I "needed help" circulating through the mothers' network at that very moment?

"*You* don't think I need 'help,' do you?" I asked Beth.

"Give me a break. I told you that I *know* there's got to be a very good reason you poked Brian."

I breathed a sigh of relief.

"What exactly was the reason?" I could tell Beth was dying to hear the whole story, so I broke down and told her why I did what I did to Brian. It surprised me that she didn't appear too shocked.

"You know, Rissa," she said after considering the facts. "It might be possible that Brian *was* going to kiss you. You know he's always had a big crush on you."

"No way."

"Yes, way. That's why we always teased you about him. We kind of thought you liked him, too."

"Yeah, right." I could feel myself blushing.

Beth dug in her pocket and produced a wad of bills. "Do you want a smoothie?" she offered. "I think I have enough money."

"I'll just have a Coke," I said.

After we got drinks, Beth and I stayed in the food court for another half hour or so, catching up on everything that had been going on. There were some things I could tell her that I couldn't tell Violet, like why I lied about Mary Ann's chosen career and how I was getting frustrated trying to learn violin and how I had mixed feelings about Mom starting a career.

It wasn't exactly like old times, but it was good. We might have stayed at our table until the mall closed if two things hadn't happened almost at once. First Beth's cell phone went off, and it was her mother telling her to go to the north entrance of the mall. Then there was an announcement on the intercom, requesting that "Clarissa Bartholomew meet her party at the *south* entrance."

WATCHING MYSELF GROW UP

On the way home from the mall, Mom was too distracted to be mad at me for running off to the food court with Beth. She didn't say anything about her argument with Mrs. White, but I could tell it was weighing on her mind. Things were weighing on my mind, too. The whole thing about Mom getting a job. The shock of knowing the truth about my birthday party. What Beth had told me about her mother thinking I needed a therapist.

With everything that happened, Mom and I hadn't gotten a chance to get fabric for my skirt, and I decided I'd better mention it when we stopped at a red light.

"Mom?"

"Hm?" It was hard to gauge her mood.

"What about my skirt?"

She looked at me blankly, then turned her eyes back to the road. "Shoot. I knew we were forgetting something."

"It's okay. My recital isn't for another two weeks. That's plenty of time, right?"

"It should be." Mom bit her lip, making me feel a little less confident about our plan. I supposed if worse came to worst, I could wear my sweater with my dyed-black pants.

"We can go back tomorrow. I guess it would make sense to decide what kind of skirt you want me to make before we buy the material," Mom continued. "Were you thinking long or short? I think something in-between would be best."

"I don't know."

I could almost see Mom's thoughts shift from Beth's mother to fashion as she began rattling off ideas for skirts. The possibilities seemed endless.

"You could sketch a picture of what you want when we get home," she said, noticing my confusion.

✿　✿　✿

While I was upstairs putting away my new sweater and bras, Mom yelled up for me to grab her sketchbook.

"There should be a new one on the shelf of my closet. It can be yours if you want it."

Flattered that Mom thought me worthy of having my own sketchbook, I hurried to her room and reached up high in her closet. I could see the edge of a book, but it was just out of reach. I gave a little jump and brushed my hand against it. It fell, and so did a pile of other spiral-bound pads of assorted sizes.

"What happened?" Mom shouted from downstairs.

"Nothing."

I reached down to gather the books, but my curiosity got the better of me. I picked one up and looked through it, finding pages and pages of sketches. Were *all* of these books filled with my mother's pictures? I put down the one in my hand and picked up another one. This time I lingered over the fashions I saw.

The girls in the pictures (most of whom had short, curly hair like me) seemed to grow progressively older, or at least their outfits got more sophisticated. Styles became more fitted. Sleeves got less puffy. Ruffles and bows were replaced with scarves and belts. It was like I was watching a more fashionable version of myself growing up.

"Did you find it? Oh, I guess you did." Mom was suddenly in the room, eyeing the mess I'd made.

"These are really good," I said, feeling a little dazed. "When did you do all of these drawings?" I looked at my mom and wondered how it was possible that I'd never seen these books before and didn't even know she'd kept on sketching long after she stopped sewing.

"Off and on over the years. But recently, I've been feeling

particularly inspired." She came over to me and began stacking the pads.

"How come you kept it a secret?" I asked.

"I didn't mean to." Mom looked startled. "It just never occurred to me to mention it. I didn't know you'd be interested."

"You should make some of this stuff. I mean, you really *could* open a boutique," I said, taking another look at a teenaged version of me wearing a minidress and black leggings.

Mom stopped stacking.

"Having my own store would take a lot of work, but maybe someday I'll do it. We'll see."

I looked back down at the sketchbook, and thought about how I liked, *really* liked some of the outfits I'd seen.

"If you ever feel like making me something again — I mean, besides the recital skirt — I might wear it," I offered.

"Thanks, but I think I'd like to work on some other things first." Mom got a dreamy look in her eyes, and I'd never felt so far away from her and so close to her at the same time.

CHAPTER 28

NOVEMBER WEARS ON

My grandmother Bartholomew has this saying:
"Time heals all wounds." I don't know if I believe it or not,
but it was true that things did get better as November wore
on. I felt more respectful toward my mom after hearing
how she'd stood up for me at my birthday party, and I
stopped worrying that she felt lonely and useless after finding out she was practically a fashion-designer genius. We
spent a lot of time together working on my skirt, which
turned out to be amazing, much better than anything we'd
seen in the stores. It was soft and silky with tiny blue flowers the same color as my new sweater, and the best thing
about it was that it had a double-layered hidden pocket big
enough (and strong enough) to hold Nicholas. He could
stay right with me during my recital and give me pep talks
if I got scared.

Dad kept asking me if I wanted to continue taking violin lessons after the recital, but I hadn't made up my mind. There were some things I didn't like about lessons, like how my progress was so slow, and how Mr. Keesly's dog whined when I hit wrong notes. But I did like the feeling of getting something right — like my bow hold — after struggling and struggling.

Other than Dad bugging me to make up my mind, things were fairly peaceful at home, and they were getting easier for me at school. Once everyone got used to seeing Brian on crutches and realized he wasn't planning revenge or anything, gossip about his "accident" started to peter out, and people got interested in other things. The boys were all into basketball because team tryouts were coming up. The girls were practicing jumps and cartwheels, hoping that they'd make the cheerleading squad. Not Beth, though. I heard she lost interest after she found out the coach wasn't all that impressed with her ballet training and yelled at her for chewing gum.

There had definitely been some regrouping of herds since Angel's party. Now it seemed that Tony Morales was Angel's boyfriend, and Kerry (who got in *huge* trouble after Angel's party) drifted off to a group of girls she knew from gymnastics class. The Skimpy-top girls, Alexandra and Cassandra (who now wore sweatshirts over their tanks at

Mrs. Lucas's request), started hanging around with Brian and Kyle Jacobs. I know that sounds too weird to be true, but it really did happen.

Most of the time, I felt like an outsider looking in, but there were times I felt a part of things, like when we played dodgeball in PE, and my teammates cheered me on, and when Jayne Littleton said she "absolutely *loved*" my recital skirt (which I couldn't resist wearing to school two weeks before my recital).

Things weren't perfect. But I could always count on Violet to eat lunch with me, and I didn't dread going to school so much anymore.

Then one day when I came home from school, Mom was all pink-cheeked with excitement.

"I got the job!" she announced.

"That's great!" I said, and I think I actually patted her on the back, but butterflies fluttered in my stomach as I pictured myself wearing a latchkey around my neck.

Then things really started to change. Mornings were a madhouse with Mom and Dad both rushing to get ready for work and me getting ready for school. We fought over the bathroom, made do with cold cereal for breakfast, and I came home to a house that looked exactly the same as I left it, with dirty dishes in the sink and beds still unmade. But being the first one home wasn't as bad as I thought it would be. I still had my gnomes to keep me company, and sometimes I called up Violet to see what she was doing. It made me feel less lonely knowing she was in an empty house, too. I didn't even mind hearing a blow-by-blow account of what her knight was up to in Book Three.

One day, after Violet was done telling me how Princess Celia had been reincarnated into a bird to become the knight's protector, our conversation drifted to more down-to-earth stuff, Thanksgiving and our plans for fall break.

"We're not going to Vermont after all," Violet said sullenly. "Mom says she'll be too busy trying to fill holiday orders at the store. *Everyone* wants free-range birds."

"That's too bad. I mean, about not going to Vermont," I said, trying to push the image of Celia dished up on a Thanksgiving platter out of my mind. "My mom has to work that weekend, too." Actually, I wasn't quite sure what we'd be doing for Thanksgiving. Usually, the Whites came over to our house, but after the feud between Mom and Beth's mom, I figured we might be eating by ourselves this year.

"Maybe we can do something together over break," Violet suggested shyly. I told her I was thinking the same thing.

❀   ❀   ❀

As soon as Mom came home from work that evening, I asked her about Thanksgiving and whether we were doing anything special.

"The Whites are coming for dinner, of course," she said as though nothing at all had happened between her and Mrs. White.

"But we hardly see them anymore," I argued, thinking how awkward it was going to be to share a feast with someone who thought I needed to go to a therapist.

"That's why they're coming over. So we *can* see them," Mom explained, picking up the mail.

"So, you're not still mad at Mrs. White?"

Mom gave me a look, and I realized she had no idea I'd overheard their fight in the mall. Then there was this strained moment with her wondering how much I knew, and me pretending I didn't know anything.

"Just because you get angry at friends doesn't mean you have to give up on them," Mom finally said. "We can talk about this later if you want. Right now I need to get out of these uncomfortable clothes." She took off her shoes and padded up the stairs.

I guessed there really wasn't much more to discuss. The Whites were coming whether I wanted them to or not. I didn't think I could ever be as tolerant as my mother, but I had to admire her setting aside her disagreements with Beth's mother for the holiday, and for putting up with her many, MANY flaws for so many years. "Friendship is no molehill," Mom had said. She must have really believed it.

It was true that friendship *could* be a mountain of work, but I guessed it was worth it sometimes. I just hoped I'd be sitting next to Beth and not her mother during Thanksgiving dinner.

SMOKED TURKEY AND FRIENDS

Even though Mary Ann was home from college, and we were a whole family again, Thanksgiving vacation had a different feel from other years. Mom had to work late the night before, so Dad, Mary Ann, and I had to do most of the "prep" work ourselves.

"This is pretty weird without Mom bossing us around, telling us what to do," Mary Ann observed as we combined ingredients for stuffing. "She *is* going to be making the turkey tomorrow, isn't she?"

"Actually, I'm going to try smoking the turkey outside," Dad told her. He'd bought a special cooker for the occasion.

"Lord, help us all," Mary Ann muttered under her breath. She hadn't been around to see how well we'd been surviving since Mom went back to work.

❀ ❀ ❀

As usual, the Whites arrived early for Thanksgiving dinner and, as usual, we weren't nearly ready. In fact, Mary Ann was still in bed.

While Mrs. White helped Mom in the kitchen and Mr. White went outside to offer Dad barbecue tips, Beth and I decided to go out on the patio, too. The turkey was smelling pretty good, and we were getting hungry.

"It feels like winter today," Beth said, pulling her hands inside the sleeves of her sweatshirt.

"I can hardly wait until Christmas!"

"Me too!" Beth's eyes lit up and her smile got really big, and for a moment she was the old Beth again.

She shivered, but I didn't mind the cold. The chill in the air made me feel kind of excited. The change of seasons was like a promise that other things would also change. Someday, the whole thing about Brian's accident would blow over and be forgotten. My dreaded recital would come and go, and no matter what else happened, Christmas would be celebrated, spring would arrive, and I would eventually graduate sixth grade.

Despite the fact that Dad dropped the turkey on the patio and it had to be rinsed in the sink, dinner turned out pretty well. Once we were all settled at the table, things weren't nearly as tense with the Whites as I feared they might be.

Nobody mentioned my suspension or the fight between Mom and Mrs. White at Studio 99 or who was or should be going to see a therapist. Conversation was light and happy. Mostly, we just talked about what we were thankful for. Here is a list of what everyone said:

★ 1. Dad was thankful that his turkey didn't come out bloody.

★ 2. Mom was thankful for her new job.

★ 3. Mrs. White was thankful for friends and family.

★ 4. Mr. White was thankful that he could watch football after dinner.

★ 5. Beth was thankful that Christmas was only four weeks away.

★ 6. Mary Ann was thankful that she'd aced all her midterm tests and had finally decided what to do with her life. . . . Be a doctor. (Spooky, isn't it?)

When it was my turn to say what I was thankful for, I was surprised to discover that I could think of quite a few things: The way Mom had stopped nagging me; Beth and me sort of being friends again; Violet and me getting along. But I didn't want to say any of this aloud.

"I'm thankful that after my recital tomorrow, I will never have to play the 'Peanut Butter Cookie' song ever again," I told everybody. Then my mother had to explain to the

Whites what that meant. And my dad reminded me once again that my three-month trial period for violin lessons was up, and I had to make a decision SOON.

Beth and I finished eating long before our parents and Mary Ann were done, so we were assigned the duty of pie cutting. While we were in the kitchen, making a general mess out of Mrs. White's lemon meringue, Violet called to see if I could come over.

Beth heard me explain to her that we had company, and whispered, "Why don't you invite her over here?"

"Are you sure?" I mouthed back. The Whites usually spent the whole day with us. Having Violet over while they were still here could be really awkward. On the other hand, it *might* work out.

"Go on, ask her," Beth prodded.

So I did, and Violet agreed.

Feeling a little shy about the prospect of Beth and Violet being in the same house together, I thought I'd better warn Beth about what topics to avoid with Violet.

"There are some subjects you won't want to bring up," I warned.

"Like what?" Beth put the last piece of pie on a plate.

"Like medieval history. Just don't ask her to do her jester dance," I pleaded. "And don't ask her if she's read any good books lately."

"Why not? Do you think I'm going to make fun of her?"

"No, it's just that I don't want anyone to be rolling their eyes or giggling at the wrong times or anything."

"For goodness' sake, I'm not an idiot. What kind of person do you think I am?"

Not a jerk, I suddenly realized.

I have to admit that Beth did really try to be nice to Violet that afternoon. She was very polite about reminding Violet when it was her turn to roll the dice when we were playing Monopoly. And although it was kind of annoying that Violet refused to trade properties, Beth didn't make a fuss, and she didn't bring up the subject of boys or hairdos once.

I could tell that Violet was making an effort, too. And even though she did go on a little too long about the Magic Castle Club and her trips to medieval fairs, she at least was making conversation, and when she gazed longingly at the books on my shelf, she stopped herself from going over there to pick one up to read it.

For the most part, everything was going very smoothly. I kind of got this warm feeling about Violet and Beth both being my friends and getting along so nicely. And I sort of wish I could just end my story here, but as you probably know, perfect moments never last forever. Mine ended right after I bought Boardwalk.

For some reason, that was the moment when Violet brought up the subject of her friend Mandy and how they used to play duets. Beth (who maybe needed a little rest from Violet's discussion of her hobbies) jumped in to ask — actually, beg me — to tell her all about my violin recital.

There wasn't much to tell. Besides, I was busy counting my money. So Violet continued talking.

"You must be really nervous about playing in front of a bunch of people," she speculated.

I looked up from my counting. "Not really," I lied. "I'm only going to be playing for about sixty seconds. What could go wrong?"

"My friend Mandy always used to get nervous before she performed. One time, one of her violin strings broke during her recital."

Beth's eyes got wide, and suddenly there was tension in the room.

"What happened then?" I asked warily.

"She didn't know what to do, so she just stopped playing, and the pianist kept right on going without her. She was mortified."

"Don't worry, that won't happen to you," Beth tried to reassure me, handing me the Boardwalk card.

"What do you mean, her string broke?" I said, slapping down Boardwalk on top of my other properties. Strings couldn't break, could they?

"It just broke. Hasn't that ever happened to you when you were practicing? It used to happen to Mandy all the time."

"My strings don't break."

"I'm sure your dad buys you extra strong strings," Beth piped in, trying to be helpful, I guess.

That's when Violet finally caught on that she was making me upset and quickly let me know the odds were very small that I would have a disaster during my performance. But it was too late. The idea of me making a great big fool of myself was planted in my head.

There were several seconds of silence. Then Violet broke it.

"Is it okay if I come to your recital?" she asked in a very small voice.

"I guess so," I mumbled, still seeing myself on stage with violin strings popping every which way.

"I'm coming, too, and so are my parents," Beth said cheerfully.

"Is it all right if my parents come, too?" Violet asked.

Why not invite the whole world? I wanted to say, but I followed Beth's lead of acting polite and told Violet that her parents would be welcome.

CHAPTER 30

THE RECITAL

If bringing Beth and Violet together at my house for Thanksgiving gave me a brief feeling of warmth, bringing them together for my recital did not. In fact, there were a lot of guests in the audience I wished were someplace else.

Have you ever been to one of those awkward parties that's full of people who don't mix very well? Maybe your grandmother is there, so you feel self-conscious hanging around with your friends. Or maybe a friend from out of town is visiting, and she doesn't get along with your other friends. Or maybe your parents give you a surprise party and invite the wrong people. Or maybe you have a party at Dino's Pizzeria and end up spending two hours in the bathroom. Okay. I'll stop there, but I just wanted you to know that my recital was one of those situations.

The little chapel where it was being held was full of people who made me anxious. I guess it was okay that my parents were there. They belonged. So did Mary Ann. She'd heard me play "Peanut Butter Cookie" and "Twinkle" about a million times, so she knew what to expect. It was the other guests who were giving me butterflies in my stomach.

The Whites (all three of them) were sitting near the front. I was afraid that if I messed up, Beth's mother would think it was because I was emotionally disturbed and Beth would feel all awkward and avoid me afterward.

Then there was Violet, who was sitting in the middle section. I had this creepy feeling that she was mentally willing my violin strings to break to prove her point that they *could* break. I know that sounds really stupid, but you can see what frame of mind I was in. To make things worse, Violet's parents *did* end up coming with her. Dr. Hayes and his wife probably expected a lot from their daughter's friend. And that made me even more tense.

I looked over my program, hoping to calm myself. That's when I saw Brian Bailey's name listed last on the sheet of paper. My stomach lurched as I scanned the backs of heads and eventually found him in the first row, sitting next to Mr. Keesly. What was he doing taking violin lessons from my teacher? Why didn't I know this?

I imagined a big, black cloud floating above my head. Brian Bailey being in my recital was like a sign from God or something. You can imagine some of the scenes that started running through my mind: Brian being shocked that I was a horrible violin student. Brian gazing up at me with his big, brown, sad eyes, wondering what he had done to deserve having his foot broken by me. Brian sneaking up behind me and pushing me down the altar stairs to get even with me pushing him off the stage. All right, I realize I was getting a little carried away, but I was in a panic.

Mr. Keesly had begun calling students up to tune their instruments. I think my heart was beating about a million times a minute when I walked up the aisle and stood there stupidly about three feet away from Brian, with the violin still under my arm. Should I say something to him? I pretended I didn't see him.

"Loosen up a little," Mr. Keesly advised, taking hold of the violin and lifting my elbow. I watched him bow my A string and tighten it a little. *String, if you're going to break, do it now and get it over with,* I silently urged. It stayed intact.

Like a robot, I walked back down the aisle, staying focused on the red exit sign. I walked past Brian and did not dare look at him. I walked past the White family. I walked past the pew where Violet and her parents were seated. Every muscle in my body wanted to keep pushing me forward out the door and down the stairs to the ladies' room. But I forced my legs to stop moving and I made my body turn when I reached my family.

"Are you all ready?" My mother asked as I slid in next to her.

"No. I think I'm going to throw up."

"No, you're not."

"And I think my violin strings are wound too tightly. One of them is going to break."

"The only thing wound too tightly is you," my mother whispered.

"I'm not kidding. I think I'm going to be sick."

Mom grabbed my arm. At first I thought she was going to take me to the bathroom, but she stayed put.

"Listen." She gave my arm a little squeeze. "Your father has paid forty dollars a week for your lessons. You will not throw up. You will not break a string. You will do a fantastic job and give your dad his money's worth."

I have to admit that it was kind of nice to hear a bit of my old mother rising up in a time of crisis. It brought me back to earth.

✿　✿　✿

I was scheduled to go third out of fifteen students. Obviously, we were going from worst to best. I remember nothing about the first two performers except that they both looked to be under the age of five.

When it was my turn to go up to the altar to perform, my throat was completely parched and my hands were damp with sweat. I kept my eyes on the red carpet of the sanctuary as I made my way down the aisle and up the stairs. My eyes were still looking down as I placed my violin under my chin and waited for Mr. Keesly's introduction on the piano.

✿　✿　✿

My versions of "Peanut Butter Cookie" and "Twinkle, Twinkle, Little Star" may have lacked expression, but the way I managed to hit the right notes earned me a hearty round of applause. And none of my strings broke. When I took a bow at the end of the song, I felt a tremendous rush of relief and was able to actually look at the audience (well, everybody except Brian) for the first time. I expected my family to be smiling up at me, but it was really nice to see Violet and Beth smiling, too. And Mrs. White gave me the thumbs-up sign. Dazed, I left the stage.

Once I was nestled back between Mary Ann and my mom, I could finally relax and watch the other students be nervous. Much to my surprise, there were some kids who messed up, and the world didn't come to an end or anything. Nobody in the audience seemed to care. Then finally it was Brian's turn. I expected him to be good since he was last, but I didn't expect him to be so absolutely amazing, which he was.

When he hobbled up onstage on his crutches and took a seat (he was the only student allowed to sit), my heart, which had been bouncing all over the place not so long ago, suddenly stood still. Brian could play. I mean, *really* play. I didn't know sounds like that could come out of a violin. Sometimes it sounded like there were two violins, not one. And he made it look so easy. It was almost like the violin was part of his body as he swayed back and forth in time to the music. How could someone as bulky and sweaty and temporarily crippled as Brian look so graceful? I wondered. But he did look graceful, and the suit he wore made him look older (and thinner). He'd just gotten a haircut, too, I noticed, and the way the light hit his head made his hair look really shiny.

Brian's piece was the longest one in the whole recital, but he could have gone on playing forever as far as I was concerned. I think other people felt that way, too, because when he stood up from his chair to take a bow, the audience exploded with applause. A few people shouted, "Bravo!"

✿ ✿ ✿

After the recital was over, I had this kind of floaty feeling as I followed the crowd into the reception room, where cookies and punch were being served. My thoughts were still on Brian's music as the adults I knew clustered around to congratulate me on my performance.

I didn't really start focusing on what was going on until Beth and Violet came over to me to give me a cup of punch.

"Well, you survived it," Beth said.

"And none of your strings broke," Violet noted. I sort of expected her to say something about her friend, Mandy, being centuries ahead of me in music, but she didn't.

"I bet if you keep working at it, you'll play like Brian Bailey someday," she said instead, and I took this as a compliment rather than an insult. The truth was that I *was* feeling inspired. Heck, if I could survive the first three months of sixth grade despite all my many disasters, there was no telling what else I might accomplish.

Dad came my way with a stack of cookies. I thought he was going to pass them out to us, but it turned out they were for himself.

"So, what's the story? Have you made up your mind about lessons yet?" he asked. "I need to let Mr. Keesly know."

"Yeah. I guess I'll keep taking them."

"Good decision. Here, have a pea-nut-but-ter-cook-ie." He handed me one off his plate.

I rolled my eyes and took a bite. While I was chewing, Beth leaned in close to me and whispered in my ear, "This is your chance to talk to Brian. Go." I looked over to where she was pointing and saw that Brian had broken away from his crowd of admirers. He was hobbling out of the reception hall by himself. "Go," Beth repeated, and gave me a little push.

I knew it was now or never.

I stuffed the rest of my cookie in my skirt pocket next to Nicholas, and called, "Brian! Wait up." He glanced over his shoulder and waited for me to catch up instead of bolting, much to my relief. "I just wanted to tell you that you did a great job," I said breathlessly.

"Thanks."

"And . . ."

And what?

"And aren't your armpits getting sore from your crutches?"

"No. I've gotten pretty used to them."

"Oh." Mentally, I was banging my head against a wall for asking such a stupid question.

"I've got to go back into the sanctuary to get my violin."

"Can I go with you?" My courage was growing now that I realized Brian wasn't going to yell at me or run away from me even if I deserved both those things. "I mean, could we talk for a minute after you get your violin?"

Brian looked at me questioningly, probably wondering if this was some sort of trick that would cause him further physical injury.

"Yeah, sure. I guess we could talk," he said cautiously.

We went back into the sanctuary, which was empty now, and headed for the first pew. I could see his battered violin case lying open.

"What did you want to talk to me about?" he asked as he closed his case.

I took a deep breath. "I just wanted to say that I'm sorry for what I did to you on Halloween. I didn't mean to make you fall off the stage. And if there was anything I could do to take it back, I would." There. I'd said it. Maybe not very grandly, but I'd said it.

Brian sat down next to me in the pew.

"It was no big deal," he said. Of course it was. He knew it and I knew it.

"But I broke your foot," I reminded him. As if he could forget.

"No, you didn't. You poked me. I broke my own foot, but I still don't get why you poked me with that flashlight. When I lifted up my helmet, there you were, looking all freaked out. I was going to ask you what was going on. Then you hit me. What did I do?"

"Nothing." I knew Brian was expecting me to say more. "Brian, this is really hard for me to explain. I can't look at you while I say it."

"Look at the wall, then."

I looked at the wall and focused on a mural of angels looking down at me with big, sad eyes. What was the worst thing that would happen if I told Brian everything? I wondered. I guess it would be that Brian would laugh at me and tell everyone at school what an idiot I was. Could I live with that? Probably.

"This is the thing," I told him. "I thought you were going to kiss me." I waited for Brian to snicker or crack a joke. He didn't. Finally, I dared to look his way, and his face was full of disbelief. Then, very slowly, he started to smile.

Finally, he said, "Cool."

Cool?

"No girl except my grandmother ever thought I was going to kiss her. . . . So, you think of me as the kind of guy who might do that?"

"Um, I don't know." Brian was confusing me. This wasn't the reaction I thought I'd get for apologizing. His chest kind of puffed out a bit and he still had that little smile on his face like he was proud of himself or something. "Anyway, I just wanted you to know that I don't hate you or anything, and making you fall off the stage was a *complete* accident."

"Breaking my foot did have some advantages. It got me a lot of attention."

I thought of the Skimpy-top girls huddled around Brian's cast.

"I just hope you're not too mad at me," I said. I was hoping he'd say that he wasn't, but just then, Mr. Keesly came up the aisle.

"Another spectacular performance." He patted Brian on the back. "You were very good, too, Rissa," he added kindly.

"Thanks, Mr. Keesly," I said.

"Thanks, Grandpa," Brian said.

Grandpa?

"You guys are related?" I looked at Brian. Then I looked at Mr. Keesly. There was a slight (and I mean *very* slight) resemblance. Then it hit me. I knew where I'd seen Mr. Keesly before I started taking lessons from him. It was at my birthday party. He had been at Dino's Pizzeria with Brian and Mrs. Bailey that day.

After Mr. Keesly left the sanctuary to say good-bye to all the parents, Brian and I stayed in the first pew and talked about some stuff — good stuff that didn't have anything to do with Halloween or awkward falls. He offered to help me practice violin sometime. He told me about this "strings camp" he was going to in the summer and said if I went, too, I'd probably be good enough for the school orchestra next year.

After a few minutes, we walked back to the reception hall together. Most people had gone home by then. The only people left were ones who were in some way connected to me. For a second, everything and everybody seemed out of place. It was like everyone was with the wrong partner. Mr. White and my dad were listening to a funny story Brian's mother was telling. Mrs. Hayes was telling Mrs. White a recipe. Mary Ann was talking to Dr. Hayes about medical school. Violet and Beth were whispering about something, and my mother came over to us and asked Brian if his mother still did volunteer work at the Salvation Army. It was all so weird. Everybody was happy and getting along. Just like they were a part of one great big herd. *My* herd.

Maybe not forever, but for this afternoon at least.